309260

INVISIBLE!

Also available by Robert Swindells,
and published by Doubleday/Corgi Yearling Books:

ABOMINATION
DRACULA'S CASTLE
HYDRA
INSIDE THE WORM
JACQUELINE HYDE
ROOM 13
NIGHTMARE STAIRS
TIMESNATCH

Published by Corgi Books, for older readers:

STAYING UP

INVISIBLE!

ROBERT SWINDELLS

DOUBLEDAY
LONDON · NEW YORK · TORONTO · SYDNEY · AUCKLAND

TRANSWORLD PUBLISHERS LTD
61–63 Uxbridge Road, London W5 5SA

TRANSWORLD PUBLISHERS, C/O RANDOM HOUSE (AUSTRALIA)
PTY LTD
20 Alfred Street, Milsons Point, NSW 2061, Australia

TRANSWORLD PUBLISHERS, C/O RANDOM HOUSE (NZ) LTD
18 Poland Road, Glenfield, Auckland, New Zealand

DOUBLEDAY CANADA LTD
105 Bond Street, Toronto, Ontario M5B 1Y3

Published 1999 by Doubleday
a division of Transworld Publishers Ltd

A catalogue record for this book is available
from the British Library

ISBN 0 385 408552

Set in 14/18pt Palatino by
Falcon Oast Graphic Art

Printed in Great Britain
by Mackays of Chatham Plc, Chatham, Kent

CHAPTER 1

'D'you want to see something special, Carrie?'

'Like what?' School was over for the day and Carrie wanted to go home. Besides, Rosie Walk was the new girl and Carrie wasn't sure she wanted her for a friend.

'I'm not telling. You've got to come with me if you want to see.'

'Where to?'

'Just the field.'

'There's nothing on the field except goalposts and dandelions and I can see them from here.'

'There's something else, Carrie. Something you wouldn't believe.'

'Oh sure. An alien craft, I bet.' She turned to

leave. Her twin brother Conrad had gone ages ago. Mum liked them to walk home together.

'Better than an alien craft. Tons better.'

'Oh yeah?' She hesitated, curious in spite of herself. She'd heard Rosie was the daughter of travellers and travellers are different. Perhaps she *had* found something on the school playing field that none of the kids had spotted. She sighed. 'OK, where is it?'

Rosie grinned and set off across the grass, which was kept short for games except round the very edge and at the four corners, where dande-lions peeped through long blades which trembled in the breeze. Carrie followed, half angry because she'd let Rosie persuade her. *It's probably something really boring, like a hole the boys have dug or a dead bird. I'll slosh her if it's anything like that.*

'Here, see.' Rosie had waded into the triangle of long grass in the farthest corner and was look-ing down at something. Carrie joined her.

'What?'

'This. D'you see the little toadstools?'

'Sure I see them. Is that it – a bunch of toad-stools? I don't call that special.'

'No, but see how they're growing in a ring, Carrie. We call it a fairy ring.'

Carrie scoffed. 'So do we. So does everybody. It's a load of rubbish. I'm off.'

'No, wait a minute. I want to show you what a fairy ring can do.'

'Do? It can't do *anything*, Rosie, except sit there.'

'You're wrong, Carrie. Watch.' Rosie placed a foot on the ring, then brought her other foot behind so that the toe of that shoe touched the heel of the first. Then she lifted the first foot and placed it behind the other, which then rose and repeated the movement. In this way, Rosie walked backwards round the ring, very care-fully, arms outstretched for balance. Carrie watched, thinking, *Big deal. She's walking back-wards. I can do that without a fairy ring.*

She was about to turn away in disgust when something astounding happened. It was so incredible that her mind refused to accept it. She screwed up her eyes, shook her head and looked again. Rosie's jumper and skirt, socks and shoes were exactly where they'd been a second ago, but Rosie was no longer inside them. Where her head should be there was nothing. Her hands were gone too, and her thin brown legs. Her clothes were hanging in mid-air. Carrie screamed.

CHAPTER 2

'Carrie, it's all right.'

It didn't *feel* all right: a school outfit without a wearer, a voice with no mouth. Carrie crammed the knuckles of her right hand in her own mouth to keep from screaming again. *If it comes towards me, I'm off.*

'Don't be scared, Carrie. Keep watching.' The black shoes reversed their direction, walking forward; heel to toe, heel to toe round the ring, as carefully as when Rosie had walked backwards. The grey skirt and maroon jumper moved too, seeming to hover above the shoes and socks. The spectacle exerted a ghastly fascination which kept Carrie rooted to the spot when her every instinct screamed at her to flee. And when the circle was complete there was Rosie, grinning as she let her arms fall to her sides. 'Good, eh?'

Carrie took her hand away from her mouth and wiped it slowly down the side of her skirt. Common sense was already asserting itself, telling her that what she thought she'd witnessed hadn't really happened. *It's a trick of some sort. Has to be.*

'How . . . how did you do that?'

Rosie stepped out of the ring. 'It's the circle, Carrie. The magic circle. Anybody can do it. Any *child*, I mean.' She smiled. 'Grown-ups can't. That's the best part about it.'

Carrie shook her head. 'I don't believe you. What is it, Rosie – hypnotism? Did you hypnotize me?'

'No, of course I didn't. I'm not that clever. It's absolutely true that if you walk backwards round a fairy ring, you become invisible.' She shrugged. 'Doesn't need to be a fairy ring. There are stone circles that'll do instead, like the one above the village.'

'Inchlake Ring?'

'Sure. Kids did it there three thousand years ago.'

'Have *you* done it there?'

'Not yet, but I will. You can too if you want to.'

'I . . . couldn't I try now, in this ring?'

'Sure, but . . .'

'But what?' *I knew it. She tricked me somehow.*

'Well the thing is, you don't become invisible *to yourself*, Carrie. You'll still see your hands and knees and you won't *feel* any different, but you'll be invisible to me.' She shrugged again. 'Means you'll have to take my word that it's worked for you, that's all.'

It's a trick. She has a good laugh while I make a prat of myself, tottering round the fairy ring with my arms out, then tells me I'm invisible. Well OK, if she's that hard up for something to laugh at. There are no witnesses. If she grasses me up to the kids tomorrow, I'll deny it. Who're they going to believe – me, or the new kid? 'All right, I'm ready.'

Rosie nodded. 'Fine. Just step into the ring and do as I did. Be careful. If any part of your foot breaks the circle, it won't work.'

'Right.'

It was harder than she'd expected, walking

backwards in a tight circle. A couple of times she nearly overbalanced. And Rosie was right about not feeling anything. She didn't realize she'd completed the circle till the other girl cried out, 'There – you've done it!'

'Have I?' She stopped, looked down at herself and saw what she always saw. *Well – what did you expect? She's having you on, you dork.* 'What do I look like?'

Rosie grinned. 'You don't look like anything, Carrie. There's just your clothes.'

Yeah, I bet. 'What if I step out of the circle now?'

'You'd stay invisible, but I wouldn't if I were you. Not here. Not in daylight. Somebody might come.'

'Right. So you want me to walk forward now, round the ring?'

'Yes. Carefully. Don't want to stay like that, do you?'

You think you're fooling me, but you're not. I'm calling your bluff. 'Rosie?'

'What?'

'Do it again, and this time I'm gonna stand right *there*.' Carrie's sleeve pointed to a spot very close to the ring. 'Let's see you vanish when I can practically *touch* you.'

Rosie nodded. 'Fine. You can shut your eyes if you want, then you can't be hypnotized.' She smiled. 'Walk forward now. Two more steps. there.' They swapped places. Rosie walked backwards. Carrie avoided the traveller's eyes but didn't close her own. She was determined to watch Rosie every inch of the way.

It happened just like before. One second she was there, the next she was not. They hadn't locked eyes so it wasn't hypnotism, and there was no way Rosie could've slipped out of her clothes and hidden in the long grass.

Carrie reached out. 'Give me your hand.' She winced as a hand slipped into hers. An invisible hand. She swallowed. 'Yes, OK. Look, would you . . . ?'

'What?' Rosie chuckled. 'Suspicious character, aren't you?'

'I suppose I am, but it's so *weird*. What I was going to ask was, would you show Con tomorrow? My brother?'

'Sure, if you like.'

'Thanks. I'd better go. Mum goes mad.'

'OK. See you, Carrie.'

'See you, Rosie. If you're not invisible, I mean.'

CHAPTER
3

When Carrie got home her twin was upstairs as usual, playing games on his computer. She knocked on his door. 'Can I come in a minute, Con?'

'What for? I'm busy.'

'I've got something to tell you.' She depressed the handle and pushed the door open.

Conrad swivelled the office chair, scowling. 'I said I was *busy*, Carrie.'

'I can't talk about this in front of Mum and Dad, Con.'

'Why not?' He looked at her. 'What you done – *murdered* somebody?'

'Don't be stupid. It's private, that's all.'

'Aw, all right.' He sighed, killed the sound FX and gave her his full attention.

Carrie told him everything that had happened on the field. When she'd finished he shook his head. 'You're a nut, Carrie. She's having you on. Invisibility's just in stories. It's a scientific impossibility.'

'I *saw* it, Con. She was there, and then she wasn't. Just her uniform, hovering over the ring. And when she reversed the action she re-appeared. I was only two metres away. I saw it happen.'

Conrad snorted. 'Know what *I* think? I think the pair of you have cooked up this tale hoping to make a donkey out of me, but it won't work. You'll have to find somebody else to play your trick on. Somebody less intelligent.' He swivelled his chair, restored the sound and plunged back into his game.

Boys! Carrie considered pulling the plug on the computer, decided against it and left the room, slamming the door.

CHAPTER 4

'You heard Mum, Carrie. *Walk home together*, she said, *not twenty minutes apart like yesterday*. So come on.'

'No. I want you to see what I saw, *then* you can call me a nut.'

Rosie sighed. 'Make your minds up, for goodness' sake. I'm expected home too, you know.'

Carrie glowered at her twin. 'I've made mine up. It's him.'

Rosie studied the boy. 'I reckon he's chicken.'

'I am *not*. 'Course I'm not, but I'm not stupid either. Nobody can be invisible.'

Rosie shrugged. 'Come and prove me a liar, then.'

'You *are* a liar.'

'Prove it.'

Conrad scowled at her. 'All right, but I warn you. When I *have* proved it, I'm going to shove so many fistfuls of grass-clippings down your neck, you'll leave a green trail all the way home.'

The girl nodded. 'Fair enough.'

'Huh!'

'OK.' Rosie had located the ring. 'Who wants to be first?' She looked at Conrad. 'What about you, since you're not chicken?'

Conrad shook his head. 'No way. I told you – I'm not stupid. You'll not catch *me* walking round a fairy ring while you have a giggle with my sister. You go first and I'll watch.' He glared. '*Very* closely.'

'Suit yourself.' Rosie stepped into the circle and walked backwards, slowly, arms outstretched.

Carrie swallowed and glanced at her brother. 'Are you watching?'

' 'Course I am, you turkey.'

'OK OK. No need to be rude.'

When Rosie vanished, Conrad rubbed his eyes and gaped. There were Rosie's clothes,

16

exactly as his twin had described. Clothes with nobody in them. He looked sidelong at Carrie, who caught his eye.

'Well? Am I a nut or not? If I am, you are.'

He shook his head. 'It's some sort of illusion, Sis. Has to be.' He scanned the long grass with slitted eyes. 'She's hiding. In a hole or something.'

'No I'm not.' A sleeve waved at them. 'See – I'm right here in my jumper.' One shoe left the ground, its sock a tube of grey wool. 'Look. I can balance on one foot.'

'Huh! I still say it's a trick. Let's see you come back.'

'Fine. Watch carefully.' The shoes began to shuffle forward round the circle. The grey skirt kept pace, swinging slightly. Above it drifted the maroon jumper, its empty sleeves stretched out. Conrad strained his eyes to discover some fraud: thin wires perhaps, but there was nothing. The shoes completed the circle and there were Rosie's legs and hands, her reddish hair framing an impudent grin. 'Come on then, Conrad – tell us how it's done.'

'I . . . can't.' He shook his head.

Rosie laughed. 'Wanna see your sister do it?'

He nodded. 'I suppose.'

Carrie took Rosie's place in the ring. Rosie came and stood beside the boy, whose cheeks had turned pale. She looked at him. '*Sure* you're not chicken, Conrad?'

'I'm sure.' He sounded croaky.

'It's just that you're as pasty as a chilled portion, and you clucked just now.'

'Shut your face.'

They watched Carrie vanish, heard her say, 'Have I done it?'

'You've done it,' confirmed the traveller child. 'Hasn't she, Conrad?'

'Y . . . yeah. You can come back, Sis. I believe you.'

'Am I a nut?'

'No you're not. Walk forward, for Pete's sake.' He felt sick.

Carrie reappeared and left the ring. 'Your turn, Con.'

'I know, I know. Give me a chance.' He stepped in. 'Backwards, right?'

The girls nodded.

'And it doesn't hurt or anything?'

'No.'

'And you always come back if you walk

forward? It never fails, I mean?'

'Never.'

'And you'll tell me when . . .?'

'Oh, for heaven's sake get on with it!' This from Carrie.

Conrad did what he'd seen the girls do, and duly vanished. They told him when he'd done it.

'But I can see myself, same as always,' he croaked.

'Rosie *told* you,' snapped Carrie. 'You're not invisible to yourself.'

'Oh, yeah. OK. I'm coming out.'

'Whoa!' Rosie shook her head. 'Not so fast, Conrad. You'll break the circle and stay like that for ever. Can't you just see your mum's face when your uniform walks in?'

'Don't say that!' He slowed down though. Right down. The girls were quite bored by the time he reappeared.

'So.' Rosie grinned. 'What d'you think?'

'It's OK.' Conrad nodded. 'Doesn't hurt or anything, but like . . . what's it good for?'

'Aw come *on!*' Rosie looked at him. 'Think about it. You're invisible. You can go anywhere. Dodge anyone. Get in places free. Listen in to people's conversations. It's terrific fun. I've done it millions of times.'

'Yeah, but . . .' Carrie frowned. 'What about your clothes? They don't become invisible. You'd have to . . .'

'Take 'em off, yes.' Rosie nodded. 'Why not – nobody's going to *see* you. You just don't pick a freezing day, that's all.'

Conrad looked at her. 'You said we'd be able to see each other, though.'

Rosie nodded. 'So what? Have you never seen anybody without clothes?'

''Course I have. It's just . . .'

'You get used to it in no time, believe me.'

Carrie frowned. 'What would we do with our stuff though? I mean, we can't just leave it here, can we? Someone'd find it. Pinch it, probably.'

Rosie shook her head. 'We won't do it here. We'll go up to Inchlake Ring. There's a place we can hide our stuff.'

'How d'you *know* that, Rosie? You only just got here.'

Rosie smiled. 'Inchlake Ring's famous with us travellers, Carrie. We know all the ancient places.'

'Ah. So when do we do it?'

Rosie shrugged. 'Saturday?'

Carrie nodded, smiling. 'Yes, all right. Saturday. What time?'

'Evening's best, when there's less chance of meeting people. Half six?'

'Great. I can't wait.'

Rosie looked at Conrad. 'And you – will you come?'

'I guess.' He looked unhappy.

Rosie grinned. 'We're a gang, then. A gang of three. We should have a name.'

Conrad scowled. 'Why?'

''Cause gangs always have names. How about *The Inchlake Invisibles*?'

'The Inchlake Invisibles.' Carrie tried it on her tongue. 'Yeah, that's cool. The Inchlake Invisibles. Let's call ourselves that, eh, Con?'

'If you like.'

'Well.' Rosie picked up her bag. 'I'm off home. See you tomorrow.' She turned and strolled off, a faint smile on her lips. Her secret was more than just fun. Much more. Yesterday she'd been the new girl, suspect and lonely. Today she was part of a gang. Better still, she was *leader* of the gang. She was going to be all right at Inchlake School.

CHAPTER
5

'Gimme that apple, gipsy.' Lee Kippax stuck out a blunt paw.

Rosie shook her head. 'No. And I'm not a gipsy.'

'My dad says you are. He says you steal and leave muck everywhere.'

'Me?'

'People who live in caravans. Gimme the apple.'

'Get lost.'

'Hand it over, or I'll . . .'

'What's the trouble?' A boy who was passing paused and eyeballed Lee Kippax.

'Shove off, Bunny,' growled the bully. 'It's none of your business.'

The boy looked at Rosie. 'Is he bugging you?'

'He's after my apple.'

'Is he?' The boy tutted, shaking his head. 'Don't you know that's stealing, Kippax?'

'I told you to shove off.'

The boy patted his pocket. '*I've* got an apple you're welcome to, Kippax.' He smiled. '*If* you can take it from me.'

'I don't want yours, I want the gipsy's.'

'You're chicken, Kippax. Go peck some corn.'

'I *told* you to . . .'

'Make me.' The boy raised his fists. 'Come on, chicken. Show us how hard you are.'

'Ah!' The bully shook his head and turned away. 'You're not worth it, Bunny. Trust you to stick up for a gipsy.' He glanced at Rosie. 'I'll see you later, kid.' He strolled away.

'What a nasty boy,' murmured Rosie, gazing after him.

The other boy nodded. 'I can't stand him. Made my life a misery when I started here.'

'How?'

'Oh, it was my name. He was forever making fun of my name. Wouldn't leave it alone.'

'Why – what *is* your name?'

The boy smiled sadly. 'You won't believe me if I tell you.'

'Try me.'

'It's Peter Rabbit.'

Rosie giggled. 'It *isn't*.'

'Told you you wouldn't believe me, but it *is*.' He pulled a face. 'Mum's sense of humour. Marries a guy called Rabbit, calls her kid Peter. I'll have my revenge someday.' He looked at Rosie. '*Are* you a gipsy?'

She smiled. 'Not exactly. Mum and Dad are what's called New Age travellers.'

'Ah.' Peter nodded. 'I've heard of them. Whose class are you in?'

'Miss Blackwell's.'

'Hey – me too.'

'Haven't seen you.'

'No, I've been off all week. Flu. You must've started Monday.'

'Yes, I did.'

'Where were you before?'

'Place called Pilgrim. It's near Glastonbury.'

The boy whistled. 'That's a long way off. So you lost all your friends?'

'Yes, but I'm used to that. I've got friends here now.'

'Who?'

'The twins, Carrie and Conrad Waugh.'

'Oh, right. They're OK.' He grinned. 'And now you've got me.'

Rosie nodded. 'Yes. Thanks for rescuing me, Peter. D'you want to join my gang?'

'You have a *gang*?'

'Well, it's just the twins and me at the moment. The Inchlake Invisibles, we call ourselves.'

'Why *Invisibles*?'

Rosie chuckled. 'You'll find out, if you're not doing much tomorrow night.'

Peter was about to pursue the matter when the nine o'clock buzzer went. He shrugged and followed the thin brown girl into school.

CHAPTER 6

Teatime Friday. The phone rang in the Waugh home. Mrs Waugh picked up, listened, then cupped the mouthpiece. 'Carrie!'

'Yes, Mum?' Carrie was upstairs, swapping her uniform for jeans and a T-shirt.

'Telephone. It's Charlotte.'

'Coming.'

'Hi, Charlotte.' Charlotte Webb was Carrie's best friend. They were both ten, but Charlotte was a Catholic and attended a different school.

'Hi, Carrie. Are you doing anything special tomorrow?'

Carrie chuckled. 'Funny you should say that.'

'What d'you mean?'

'Oh . . . nothing. D'you want to meet?'

'I thought we might check out Sizzlers. See who turns up.' Sizzlers was Inchlake's only burger joint. A lot of kids went there Saturdays.

'Fine. I've nothing on till evening.' A stray thought entered her head, making her giggle. *I'll have even less on then.*

'What's funny?'

'Nothing. I'm in a daft mood, that's all. Take no notice.'

'So what time?'

'Oh . . . half ten?'

'Great. I'll see you then.'

'Sure will. 'Bye Charlotte.'

''Bye, Carrie.'

Carrie went upstairs and knocked on Conrad's door. He was on the computer as usual.

'What?'

'Can I come in?'

'I suppose.'

She sat on the bed. 'Charlotte just phoned.'

'So?'

'We're meeting in the morning. Sizzlers. I wondered if I should tell her about . . . you know?'

Her twin shook his head. 'No. It's Rosie's thing, isn't it? She might not be too pleased if we blab to a complete stranger.'

'Charlotte's not a stranger.'

'She is to Rosie, you clown.'

'Yes, but . . .'

Conrad sighed. 'What's the use of asking me, then arguing? Tell her if you want. She won't believe you anyway. She'll think you're out of your tree.'

'I think I will. I might even ask her to meet us up at the Ring.'

'Suit yourself. I might not be there anyway.'

'You've got to come, Con. You promised.'

'No I didn't. The word promise was never spoken. Anyway I'm still thinking about it.'

'If you don't come, I'll never speak to you again.'

Her brother smiled. 'That settles it then . . . I *won't* come.'

'Pig!'

After tea Carrie lay on her own bed, thinking. *It's funny. When Rosie's there, invisibility sounds perfectly reasonable but afterwards – now, for instance – it somehow doesn't seem real. Did it actually happen or was it an illusion, like the Indian rope-trick? After all, thousands of people have watched a man climb the rope – a rope attached to nothing – then vanish into thin air, but we know it doesn't actually happen. It's a shared illusion.*

She thought about it till twilight thickened into darkness and she heard Conrad go down for his bedtime drink, but she reached no conclusion. All she knew was that whatever happened, she'd be at Inchlake Ring this time tomorrow. If invisibility was an illusion it was a good one, well worth seeing again.

CHAPTER 7

It was raining on Saturday morning and Sizzlers was busy. Carrie paused in the doorway, flipped back the hood of her jacket and peered around. Every table was taken. She was about to leave when she noticed somebody waving. It was Charlotte, who must have arrived early and bagged a corner table. Carrie waved back and made her way across, mopping her face with a tissue. Charlotte had spread her stuff on the three vacant seats to discourage others. She cleared one and Carrie sat down. 'Thanks. Rotten morning.' She balled up the sodden tissue and dropped it in the ash-tray.

'Yes. I thought we'd check out the park later but it's not fit.'

'Never mind, there's always the mall.'

'True. I want to see if Our Price has the new Split le Beau poster.'

'Oooh, *don't.*' Carrie rolled her eyes. 'You'd think they would have, wouldn't you, seeing he was *born* here?'

'Hmmm. Wish he lived here now, next door to us.'

'Fat chance – about as much chance as winning the lottery.'

'I *know.* Who'd live in Inchlake if they had a choice? Nothing ever happens.'

Carrie giggled. 'Something might.'

'How d'you mean?'

'I'm into something, Charlotte. Something amazing.'

'What sort of something?'

Carrie pulled a face. 'You're going to think I'm crazy when I tell you.'

'No I'm not. Go on.'

'OK, listen.' Carrie told her friend about Rosie, and about what she and Conrad had witnessed on the school playing field on Wednesday and Thursday afternoons. 'So,' she

31

concluded, 'we're meeting up at Inchlake Ring at half six tonight to see what it's like when we take our clothes off and become completely invisible. What d'you think?'

Charlotte toyed with her straw. 'Do you . . . do you believe it, Carrie? D'you think you really did vanish, or did this Rosie character play some sort of trick?'

Carrie shrugged. 'I don't know, Charlotte. I keep telling myself it's impossible, but I *saw* it. I saw Rosie's empty uniform, and Con's. I don't know how anyone could fool me about that.'

'Hmmm. And you're inviting me along?'

'Yes, will you come?'

'I suppose so.' Charlotte chuckled. 'I'm always moaning on about boredom, and this doesn't sound boring, even if it turns out to be nothing but a great big wind-up.'

'It's no wind-up,' said Carrie, tilting her empty can. 'Shall we have another?'

CHAPTER 8

The stones of Inchlake Ring bit into an orange sky as Charlotte and the twins climbed the grassy hill. They'd left their watches at home, but it was probably about six fifteen. Below and behind them, the village lay submerged already in shadow though the sun still shone up here. For two hundred years the footpath they trod had conducted sightseers to the ancient hilltop monument, and for centuries before that, local people had climbed the hill to enjoy the view, to picnic or to be alone with their lovers. This evening though, the children had it all to themselves.

Rosie was there when they reached the top,

sitting with her back against one of the great stones. Peter Rabbit was standing on the so-called altar stone which lay at the centre of the circle, watching the sun go down. Carrie was surprised to find him here.

'I didn't know you were bringing somebody else, Rosie.'

'I didn't know *you* were. Who's this?'

'My friend Charlotte. Charlotte, meet Rosie.'

'Hi, Rosie. Hope you don't mind me coming?'

''Course not.' Rosie looked at Carrie. 'Peter rescued me from Lee Kippax. I owed him one, so I invited him. Do you have a problem with that?'

'No-o.' Carrie pulled a face. 'It's just . . . you know. Getting undressed and that. Feels awkward.'

Rosie stood up, grinning. 'I *told* you – you'll get used to that in no time. Shall we make a start?'

'What do we do?'

'Same as the fairy ring. Stand inside the circle and walk backwards all the way round. It's a lot easier because there's so much room. You're not going to break the circle unless you're a total wuss, and we can all do it at the same time.'

'Do we take our stuff off first?'

Rosie shrugged. 'Makes no odds but I do it after, just in case someone's watching. Come on.'

Rosie and the twins got in line. Charlotte and Peter hung back. Rosie looked at them. 'What's up?'

Peter shook his head. 'You've all seen this done. I haven't. Mind if I watch first?'

Charlotte nodded. 'Same here. I'd like to see you do it before I have a go.'

Rosie nodded. 'Fine. Here we go then.'

Gasps of astonishment rose from the two watchers as the trio completed the circle and vanished.

Charlotte glanced at Peter. 'I see clothes. Just clothes. Do you?'

'Y . . . yeah. I didn't believe, you know?'

'Jesus, Mary and Joseph, nor did I. I don't know whether to stand or run away.'

'Don't run.' Rosie's voice, with a laugh in it. 'There's nothing to be scared of. We're still here. We'll take our stuff off now, put it in the hole.'

'What hole?' The voice of Conrad.

'This one over here.' The two children watched as three sets of T-shirts, jeans and trainers walked in line to where a large rectangular recess gaped at the base of a standing stone. Here, the outfits stood in a semicircle and were stripped from invisible bodies, crumpling to shapeless bundles which unseen hands thrust into the recess. Now Charlotte and Peter would have thought themselves alone, if . . .

'Rosie?' This from Peter.

'Still here.'

'Me too.' Carrie's voice.

'And me.' Conrad.

'Come on.' Rosie. 'Your turn. Doesn't hurt a bit.'

Boy and girl looked at each other. 'Shall we?' Peter sounded hoarse.

'I suppose so.' They positioned themselves beside a stone and moved backwards, slowly. Both were afraid, and their fear stretched out time so that it seemed to take forever to go right round. Presently though there came a cheer from the other three, and looking towards the sound they beheld Rosie and the twins wearing exultant grins and absolutely nothing else.

CHAPTER 9

'Have we done it?' Peter held up his hands and examined them. 'Don't look any different.'

Rosie chuckled. 'If you can see the rest of us, you're invisible. Visible people can't see us at all.'

'Yeah, well, I can *see* you all right.' Peter felt his cheeks go hot. 'In fact I don't know where to look.'

Rosie laughed. 'Well there you are, then. You can see us so you're invisible. And if you're *still* not convinced, look at your shadow.'

'Huh?' Away to the west, the sun's rim was touching the horizon. Shadows of standing stones lay long across the grass, but where

Peter's shadow ought to be there was nothing. Rosie giggled at the expression on his face. 'See? The sun's shining through you as if you weren't there. *Now* do you believe?'

'I . . . suppose so, but it's pretty embarrassing. I mean, I don't have a sister. I've never seen . . .'

'Oh come *on*, Pete. I told you – you'll soon get used to it, and we can do anything we like now we're invisible. Follow me, only watch where you put your feet.' She grinned. 'Thistles and broken glass can be disastrous to bare feet.'

She led them downhill. On the bottom stretch of the footpath, just outside the village, they saw an old man walking his Jack Russell terrier.

'Ssssh!' Rosie pressed a finger to her lips. 'No use being invisible unless you're inaudible too. The dog'll come.'

Carrie looked at her. 'Can it see us?'

'No, but it'll know we're here. Dogs go more by scent than sight.'

Sure enough, as the five children drew near the terrier gave a little yip, bounded towards them and began scampering about their feet, jumping up and whining. Its stumpy tail quivered with pleasure as first one child then another bent to ruffle its ears. The old man peered towards the scene of activity, and for an awful moment Carrie felt sure he must see them. It was only when he yelled at the dog that she knew he couldn't. 'Matty! Come 'ere, you barmy mutt – what the heck's up with you?' To him, the animal was fussing round absolutely nothing. The children clamped hands over their mouths to stifle laughter as he came stumping towards them, muttering swear words he'd never dream of using in front of children. The terrier ignored him, and Conrad had to jump back when the man made a lunge, grabbed Matty's collar and clipped on the lead. As he began dragging the dog towards the village the children capered round him, goading the unfortunate Matty into a frenzy of barking and tugging. Where the footpath gave way to a cobbled lane, Rosie made them stop. They weren't quiet enough. Only Matty's barking had prevented the old man from hearing their giggles. They'd need more practice before she'd trust them in the village.

'That was ace,' grinned Conrad as they padded uphill in deep twilight. 'Frantic dog, old guy swearing his head off. I learned four new words.'

Rosie shook her head. 'That was nothing to what we'll do later, but it's really important to keep quiet. If enough people report disembodied voices, scientists'll investigate and then *every* kid will know the secret. It won't be fun any more.'

'Brrr.' Charlotte wrapped her arms round herself. 'It's gone flipping cold since the sun went down. I want my clothes.'

Peter nodded. 'Me too.'

Rosie smiled. 'Race to the top then, OK? Winner hides everyone's stuff. Go!' She went off like a mountain goat and the others followed, too breathless to protest.

CHAPTER
10

Sunday morning, ten o'clock. Rosie opened the rear door of the old ambulance which was her home, descended by way of two metal steps and stood barefoot in the dewy grass, stretching and yawning. It was going to be a beautiful day. Hazy sunshine glowed through a mist which would soon burn off. The lightest of breezes stirred the fluffy heads on the willow herb, freeing seeds which drifted lazily beneath their parachutes, up and away. Down among the stems, spider webs glittered as the sun turned dewdrops to diamonds. Rosie breathed in deeply, her senses filtering the elusive scents of late summer.

'Good afternoon, lazybones.' Her father had carried water from the stream to boil for tea and was watching her through the steam.

She grinned. 'It's only ten o'clock.'

'Only?' He lifted the billy from the Gaz and poured. 'I've been up three hours. There's porridge if you want it.'

'Where's Mum?'

'Gone up the village for baccy.' He smiled. 'I expect she'll get you a choc bar or something, you're so spoilt.'

'I am *not*.' Rosie knelt at the bucket, scooped up icy water and splashed it on her face, scrubbing vigorously with her palms and using fingers to wash inside and behind her ears. 'Spoilt kids have hot water and central heating. I have to make do with this old bucket.'

Her father looked at her, stirring tea with a battered spoon. 'Is that what you want, Rosie? Hot water and central heating?'

She shrugged, reaching for the towel. 'Sometimes, in winter.' She rubbed herself warm and shook her tousled hair. 'No, not really. Not if it means living in one place all the time, in a house.' She draped the towel over a bush, got up and helped herself to porridge.

She'd just started eating when she heard a
vehicle approaching. It slowed, pulled off the
road and came nosing along the bit of overgrown track their home was parked on. When
he saw that it was a police car, Rosie's father got
to his feet. Not everybody liked travellers, and
sometimes a visit from the police meant trouble.

The car pulled up and two officers got
out. One of them nodded to the watchful
traveller.

'Morning.'

'Morning.' Rosie's father remained wary. 'Is
something wrong?'

'Why, sir, should it be?'

The traveller shook his head. 'Not that I know
of.'

'Well that's all right then, isn't it?' One officer,
a woman, moved off and started walking round
the ambulance as though she might be interested in buying it. The other gazed at its owner.
'I'm Detective Sergeant Springer and that's D.C.
Widmead. Can I ask you where you were last
night sir, between midnight and four a.m.?'

'I was here, sleeping. Where else would I be?'

'Where else?' The policeman pulled a face.
'*Somebody* was over by Inchlake Manor between

those hours, sir. I suppose it wasn't you, by any chance?'

'I told you – I was here.'

Rosie looked up at the officer. 'He was, and so was I and so was Mum.'

'Where's your mum now, miss?'

'Gone to the village.'

'I see.' He looked at her father. 'D'you mind telling me your name, sir?'

'Not at all. I'm Daddy Bear, and my wife is Mummy Bear.'

The officer sighed. 'Your *real* name sir, please.'

'That *is* my real name. I chose it myself. It's not against the law, you know.'

'I know the law, sir. I'll call DVLC with your vehicle registration. They'll have your – er – previous name.' He looked at Rosie. 'Baby Bear, is it?'

Rosie shook her head. 'Rosie.'

'Thank God for that.' He glanced towards his colleague, busy kicking one of the ambulance's tyres. 'Mind if we take a look inside the vehicle, sir?'

'What on earth for?'

The officer shrugged. 'You know, sir – routine.' He frowned. 'I could probably get a warrant.'

The traveller shook his head. 'That won't be necessary. Help yourselves. We've nothing to hide, only don't mess the place up. It's our home.'

'Why're they bothering us?' hissed Rosie, when the officers had disappeared inside. Her father shook his head. 'Not sure, sweetheart. Probably investigating a burglary at that place he mentioned – Inchlake Manor.'

'But why *us*, Dad? Why do people assume we're criminals, just because we travel?'

The big man shrugged. 'Who knows? It's an old prejudice. Gipsies. Tinkers. New Age travellers. We're that little bit different, you see.' He chuckled. 'People have a problem with that.'

The officers emerged after a minute or two, empty-handed. The man came over. 'Right, sir, that's all for now. You're not planning to move on in the next day or two, are you?'

The traveller shook his head. 'Not so soon, and when we *do* we're not that hard to find.' He gazed at the officer. 'We've no reason to hide, you see.'

Rosie watched the car reverse down the track and zoom off up the road. Her porridge had gone cold. She scraped it back into the pan and set it on the Gaz, scowling. She hated warmed-up porridge.

CHAPTER
11

One of the best things about Sizzlers was that it
was open on Sundays. A juicy burger with all
the trimmings makes a fine Sunday lunch,
especially if you've only had warmed-up
porridge for breakfast. The Invisibles had
arranged to meet at Sizzlers at two, but Rosie
got there early so she could eat before the others
arrived. They'd only get Cokes, having eaten
lunch at home, and she didn't want them drooling over her Big Boy two-decker cheeseburger
with fries, or her three flavours ice cream in a
tall glass with hot fudge sauce and chocolate
buttons.

She'd finished eating and the waitress had

cleared when the twins showed up. They joined her and ordered drinks, and by the time the Cokes came Charlotte and Peter were there too. Peter slid into a red plastic seat and grinned. 'You know what we should do, don't you?'

Carrie looked at him. 'What should we do, Pete?'

'We should order five of everything on the menu, scoff the lot, then go in the toilets and make ourselves invisible so we could sneak out the door without paying.'

'We'd need a ring, dummy. And what about our clothes?'

'We chuck 'em out the window, pick 'em up round the back. Easy-peasy.'

Carrie laughed. 'You're a criminal deep down, aren't you, Pete?'

Peter shook his head. 'No, not really. I was joking.'

Rosie nodded. 'I hope so, Peter. You see, there's a rule about that.'

'What d'you mean? *Whose* rule?'

'My rule. It says we never use our invisibility to do bad things, like stealing.'

Conrad looked at her. 'You mentioned getting in places free. That's the same as stealing.'

Rosie sighed. 'I didn't mean we'd actually *do* it, Conrad. I was giving examples of what's possible, that's all.'

'Oh, right.' He smiled. 'And are there any other rules, Rosie, while we're at it?'

She shook her head. 'No, just the one.'

'What if one of us breaks the rule?'

Rosie shrugged. 'Anyone who breaks the rule is out of the gang.'

'But he can still make himself invisible.'

'Yes, but you'd be surprised how little fun it is by yourself. Anyway,' she smiled, 'none of us is going to break the rule, so it doesn't matter.' Her smile faded as she continued, 'There *are* crooks about, though. Visible ones. We had a visit from the police this morning.' Briefly, she told them what had happened at breakfast-time.

When she'd finished, Charlotte nodded. 'My dad heard about it in the paper shop. They used a glass-cutter and got away with two priceless paintings.'

Conrad arched his brow. 'Priceless?'

'Well – they're worth millions. Dad says it's happening all over. A gang of art thieves, break-ing into big houses, taking pictures and statues and stuff. The cops reckon it goes to crooked collectors abroad.'

'Wow! And I thought nothing ever happened in Inchlake.'

Charlotte shook her head. 'It's not just Inchlake, Con. It's the whole area.'

'Yeah, but like . . . the gang's *headquarters* might be here, mightn't it? Hey, listen.' His eyes shone with excitement. 'We could investigate, right? *The Inchlake Invisible Detective Agency.* What d'you reckon?'

Carrie gazed at her twin. 'What do I reckon? I reckon you're barmy, Con. A total nut.' She appealed to the others. 'Am I right?'

Rosie pulled a face. 'I dunno, Carrie. Maybe, but I'll tell you what – we *could* go invisible and take a look round Inchlake Manor. Search for clues. It's something to do on a boring Sunday, isn't it?'

Peter frowned. 'There's a problem.'

Rosie looked at him. 'What?'

'Clothes. Where to take 'em off and where to hide 'em. It's Sunday afternoon and the sun's shining. That means flocks of people up at Inchlake Ring.'

'No prob.' This from Conrad.

His sister glanced at him. 'What d'you mean, no prob?'

'We're talking about the Manor, right? Well, there's an old building in the grounds. The ice house, they call it. Nobody ever goes there. We could use that.'

Rosie shook her head. 'We need a *ring*, remember.'

'It *is* a ring. The ice house, I mean. It's round. Would that work, Rosie?'

Rosie shrugged. 'One way to find out. Come on.'

CHAPTER
12

They'd expected police activity, but everything seemed quiet as the five children passed between the great granite gateposts of Inch-lake Manor. Weeds poked through the gravel of a driveway narrowed by long-neglected rhododendrons crowding in on either side. At this time of year the house lay hidden beyond a dense screen of foliage. Provided no vehicle followed them through the gateway there was little chance of their being seen.

Rosie looked at Conrad. 'Where's this whatsit then – ice house?'

'See that?' The boy nodded towards a gap in the rhododendrons. 'Through there. There's a pathway curves right round the back of the house.'

'How d'you know, Con? Ancestral home, is it?'

He shook his head. 'A bunch of us used to mess around here, exploring.'

'Ah.'

It was dark under the trees. The path was narrow, slimy and overgrown. It made Carrie think of frogs and toads, though she didn't see any. Her twin went first, leading them in a great curve till a weird structure appeared in the tangle to their right. It was shaped like an igloo but was much bigger, built with great blocks of stone. Conrad held up a hand and they stopped.

Rosie gazed at the ice house. 'Where's the door?'

'Halfway round. Careful when you go in – floor's below ground level.' He led the way round the igloo's mossy curve to a doorless entrance where he sat down, dangling his legs into darkness.

Charlotte peered over his shoulder. 'Ugh!' She shuddered. 'It's pitch-black and it stinks. I'm not going in there.'

Conrad chuckled. 'It only smells like mush-rooms, and it's not really dark once your eyes get used to it. Here goes.' He planted his palms on the rim and lowered himself, feeling for the floor with his trainers. When he dropped and turned, his chin was level with the ground.

One by one the others followed. Conrad helped them down. They stood in the light from the door-way and peered nervously into the blackness. Peter thought of monsters. Charlotte fancied she could see something moving. Conrad let out a sudden whoop whose echo was augmented by the screams and gasps of his companions.

'Daft beggar!' snarled his twin, when she'd recovered enough to speak. 'Scared me half to death.'

'And me the other half.' Peter's voice sounded hoarse.

Conrad was laughing so much he had to lean on the wall to keep from collapsing.

Very funny, Rosie thought but didn't say. *But not half as funny as what I'll do to you when you least expect it.* Aloud she said, 'Did we come here to play silly games, or do we go invisible and get on with our investigation?'

'Investigation,' voted Carrie. '*If* this place works like a stone circle.'

Rosie nodded. 'It'll work. I'll go first if you like.'

'Go on then, but I vote we keep a hand on each other's shoulders all the way round so we don't get separated. Will it be OK like that?'

'Don't see why not. Everybody set? Then let's go.'

CHAPTER
13

It worked, as Rosie had hoped it would.

They left their things on a dank ledge and scrambled out of the ice house. It felt good to breathe fresh air, though it was a bit cold. They moved slowly between the trees, careful where they put their feet. Presently the foliage thinned and there loomed the Manor, looking semi-derelict with its faded paintwork and dusty windows.

Rosie pulled a face. 'Bit of a dump, isn't it? Inchlake Manor. I expected something really posh.'

'Yeah, well.' Conrad nodded. 'It used to be posh when the family had it, but there's only the old lady left now. Miss Massingberd. She can't keep up with it.'

'Hmm.' Rosie shook her head. 'Can't imagine priceless paintings here, can you?' She frowned. 'Wonder how the thieves knew?'

They worked their way round to the front of the house, keeping to the fringe of the trees. A flight of mossy-looking steps led up to great double doors, which were closed. Somebody had parked a yellow Polo at the foot of the steps.

'Who's is that, d'you reckon?' whispered Charlotte. 'Doesn't look like a police car.'

Conrad shrugged. 'Search me.'

His twin giggled. 'That wouldn't take much doing right now, Con.'

'Shut up.'

'Let's take a closer look.' Rosie set off across the lawn. The others hung back and she turned, grinning. 'It's OK. You're invisible, remember?' They'd forgotten, which was easy when they could see each other. They followed, wearing sheepish expressions.

There was a sticker on the inside of the car's windscreen. NURSE ON CALL.

Rosie nodded. 'That explains it. District nurse. Miss Massingberd must be pretty decrepit.'

'She is,' confirmed Conrad. He looked at Rosie. 'What we gonna do?'

'Find a way in, have a snoop round.'

'You mean inside the house?'

'Sure, why not? Nobody's going to see us.'

'So we just march through the door?'

'Well, perhaps not *this* door. No point taking unnecessary risks. There'll be a side door some-where. Stay close, and no talking.'

They crept along the front of the Manor, peering into windows. Great dim rooms lay beyond the streaky panes, their furniture shrouded in sheets. Turning a corner they found a con-servatory built onto the south wall of the house and, in the angle of the wall and its cast-iron frame, a door which squealed open when Rosie tried it. Hardly daring to breathe, the Inchlake Invisibles tiptoed inside and stood on a floor of terracotta tiles, gazing around.

It seemed Miss Massingberd used the con-servatory as a sun lounge. A small table stood beside a wicker armchair. There were books and tea things on the table, crumpled cushions in the chair and a footstool nearby. It looked as though the old lady might have been sitting here until a few minutes ago. Behind the furniture an open door gave on to a dim corridor. Many of the conservatory's windows had cracks in them, and Rosie noticed that one had no glass at all but was boarded up with a sheet of plywood. The wood looked new, and Rosie wondered whether this was where the thieves had got in. She was walking towards it when Carrie hissed a warning. A door in the corridor had opened and a frail old lady was shuffling towards the conservatory, one hand hooked through the arm of a strapping nurse.

CHAPTER
14

'Freeze!' hissed Rosie. 'Not a word.'

It felt weird, standing like statues as the two women came slowly across the tiles. Impossible to believe they wouldn't be seen the instant Miss Massingberd glanced up. Or the nurse. Carrie began rehearsing an excuse. *The door was open. We were exploring. We thought it was an empty house . . .*

The nurse steered Miss Massingberd to her chair, practically brushing against Charlotte, and steadied the old lady as she sank into it. 'There.' Charlotte had to take a rapid step backwards as the nurse straightened up. 'Are you *sure* there isn't somebody who would come and sit with you? It must be a nasty shock, knowing thieves have been in your house.'

Miss Massingberd shook her head. 'Not so much a shock as a disappointment, dear.'

'Disappointment?'

'Oh, yes. You see, I had planned to sell those paintings to pay for repairs to this place. It's falling to pieces, year by year. A hundred jobs need doing and there's no money.'

The nurse looked sympathetic. 'Yes, it must take a lot of keeping up, a place like this. Weren't the paintings insured?'

'Oh no, dear. Far too expensive, insurance. They expect you to install all sorts of alarms and lights and whatnot which cost a fortune, and when you say you can't afford it they refuse to insure.'

The nurse shook her head. 'I'm sorry, Miss Massingberd, really I am.' She smiled. 'If you're sure there's nothing more I can do for you, I'd best be on my way.'

'Windows.'

'Windows?'

'Yes, windows. Or rather, their *frames*. They're the most urgent problem. Rotten wood, you see.'

'Ah – yes, I see. Well . . .'

'Practically falling out, some of them. Rattle on windy nights. One good storm and – whoosh! – they'll be gone. Then where shall we be?'

'I . . . really don't know, Miss Massingberd. I'll see you tomorr . . .'

'Man was up just a couple of days ago. Carpenter fellow from the village, what's his name? Kipper. Kepler. Something like that. I'd called him to come and inspect the frames, you see. Prepare an estimate. Well, I expected there'd be money, from the paintings. Now . . .' The old lady shrugged. 'Nothing. Not a bean. Better if I'd sold the bally pictures years . . .' She broke off and gazed at the nurse. 'Don't you have patients waiting, dear? Oughtn't you to be on your round, or whatever it's called?'

Charlotte let out a long, careful sigh as the nurse picked up her bag and departed in an antiseptic waft. *Thought she'd never go.* She looked across at Rosie, who nodded towards the door and mouthed the word *out*. Miss Massingberd's head was nodding. With visits from the police and the nurse she'd had a tiring morning, but if she'd known five invisible callers were tiptoeing past her chair, she'd have found it less easy to fall asleep.

CHAPTER 15

The five had put twenty metres between themselves and the conservatory when Carrie whistled.

'Jeez, that was scary! You don't *feel* invisible, do you?'

Peter shook his head. 'No, but you certainly feel *bare*.' He giggled. 'I kept expecting the old bird to look at me and say, *Where are your* clothes, *young man?*'

Conrad nodded. 'Me too. I couldn't believe we could just stand there and they wouldn't know.'

'What about *me*?' squealed Charlotte. 'That nurse actually brushed me with her skirt as she went past. I nearly died.'

Rosie smiled. 'You all did fine. Much quieter than last time.'

Peter scoffed. 'We flipping well *had* to be didn't we, with people two metres away.'

'Millimetres,' amended Charlotte.

Rosie nodded. 'That's another thing. You've got to make sure nobody actually *touches* you, because that's an even bigger give-away than hearing something.'

Conrad looked back at the Manor. 'Are we leaving already? We didn't do much searching for clues.'

Rosie shook her head. 'We don't *have* to leave. I thought you might have had enough, what with the scare and all. Who's for staying?'

'I'm all right,' murmured Peter.

'Me too.' This from Charlotte.

Carrie nodded. 'We're OK, Rosie. What shall we . . .' She broke off at the sudden noise of a car engine.

Rosie grinned. 'Don't panic, it's only Florence Nightingale.'

'Who?'

'The nurse, you spack. Leaving.'

'Oh. Oh yeah.'

They stood on the overgrown lawn, listening.

The engine noise receded till the wind in the grass was louder. Then they wandered back towards the house, giving the conservatory and its sleeping occupant a wide berth.

They circled the Manor, combing neglected flower-beds and peering into shrubs, finding nothing. When they reached the south wall again, Rosie advanced alone to examine the freshly boarded window and the ground under it. Through the streaky panes she could see the back of Miss Massingberd's chair and the top of the old lady's head. Traces of a silvery powder on the window frame meant the police had dusted for fingerprints. There was nothing else.

'Waste of time,' growled Peter as the five picked their way towards the ice house.

Rosie shrugged. 'Good invisibility practice, if nothing else.'

'Hope nobody's swiped our stuff,' murmured Charlotte.

'Hey.' Carrie's eyes sparkled. 'What if the thieves have hidden the paintings in the ice house?'

Her twin scowled. 'Why the heck would they do *that*, dipstick?'

'I dunno. Too heavy to carry, perhaps.

You know – come back later with a truck?'

Rosie grinned. 'Suppose they come back while we're in there, just as we go visible?'

'Oooh!' Charlotte shivered. 'Don't say that, Rosie, for goodness' sake. It's going to take me all my time to go back into that place as it is.'

The ice house lay silent under its canopy of trees. Their clothes were undisturbed. They dressed quickly, crowded into the half-light by the door. Truth was, they'd spooked themselves with talk of the thieves. They knew they had to circle once more in the inky blackness and nobody fancied it.

Halfway round, a heavy hand fell on Conrad's shoulder and a voice growled in his ear, *Gotcha, you miserable young snooper.* The boy's scream nearly blew the roof off, and it was ten minutes before he was able to complete the circle on rubber legs. Rosie had got her revenge.

CHAPTER 16

Mummy Bear plucked the pegs from a pair of jeans, folded the garment over her arm and handed the pegs to Rosie, who dropped them in the bag. A sunny day and a light breeze had dried the washing beautifully. Now, at dusk, big moths looped round the fire Daddy Bear was tending a few metres away. He'd built it downwind of the line so smoke wouldn't spoil the clean clothes. He'd cook dinner over the fire and later they'd sit round it till bedtime, talking.

'So.' Mummy Bear took down a jumper. 'What did you do today, Rosie?'

'Oh, I met some of the kids at Sizzlers.' Rosie

dropped pegs in the bag. 'We went invisible and had a snoop round Inchlake Manor.'

'You did? What for?'

'I thought we might find a clue to who burgled the place.'

'And did you?'

'I'm not sure.'

'Ah-ha.' The line was empty. Her mother dumped the last of the clothes in the basket and straightened up. 'You *are* being careful who you teach invisibility to, aren't you, sweetheart? It's a dangerous skill in the wrong hands, you know.'

Rosie nodded. 'I know, Mummy Bear. I wouldn't give it to anybody who'd use it in bad ways.'

Mummy Bear smiled. 'I know you wouldn't, Rosie. Come over to the fire and tell Daddy Bear and me all about these friends.'

'Well, there are four of them,' began Rosie, when they'd settled themselves. Daddy Bear leaned forward with a long spoon to stir the stewpot. 'Two girls and two boys. The girls' names are Carrie and Charlotte, and the boys are called Peter and Conrad. Carrie and Conrad are twins. Charlotte goes to a different school but she's Carrie's best friend. Peter saved me from a bully.'

Daddy Bear smiled through fragrant steam. 'It's good you have friends, Rosie. I bet I can guess what you're calling yourselves.'

'What?'

'The Inchlake Invisibles.'

'How'd you *know* that?'

He laughed. 'It's not that hard, sweetheart. Let's see: so far this year we've had the Pilgrim Invisibles, the Appleby Invisibles and now the Inchlake Invisibles. Last year it was the Whitby Invisibles and the Kirk Yetholm Invisibles. Next year . . .'

'Yeah, OK OK.' Rosie lifted a hand. 'I know I'm not big on originality, but what *can* you call a gang that makes itself invisible?'

Her father chuckled, shaking his head. 'It doesn't matter, honeybunch. You make friends everywhere we drag you, and *that*'s what matters. Bring 'em over one evening and we'll have a barbecue.'

Rosie grinned. 'Thanks, Daddy Bear, that'll be really cool.'

Daddy Bear smiled. 'Better do it before the end of the month or it won't be just cool, it'll be bitterly cold.' He lifted the spoon and tasted the stew. 'Mmmm. I reckon this is just about ready if you want to pass your plates.'

CHAPTER
17

'Rosemary Walk.' Miss Blackburn plucked Rosie's essay from the top of the pile and frowned at it. 'I asked everybody to write a piece entitled *My Family*. I expected *factual* pieces.' She looked at Rosie over the top of her half-moon glasses. 'You may remember we talked last week about different *sorts* of writing. Fiction was one sort. What *is* fiction, Rosemary?'

'Miss, it's made-up stories with characters instead of real people.'

'And factual writing?'

'Miss, factual writing's about real people and actual events, like history and that.'

'Correct. So why did you give me a piece

which mixes fact with fiction?'

'I didn't, miss. Everything's true that I wrote.'

'No, Rosemary, it is not.' The teacher read from the top sheet. 'I have no sisters or brothers. There's just Mum and Dad and me. My dad's name is Daddy Bear, my mum's is Mummy Bear.'

Some of the children sniggered. Miss Blackburn gazed at Rosie. 'Daddy Bear is not a name, you silly girl, and neither is Mummy Bear. Since your surname is Walk, I assume your parents are Mr and Mrs Walk. If you don't know their first names, Mr and Mrs Walk will be quite sufficient.' She skated the essay across Rosie's table. 'Corrections in the margin, please, and no more fairy tales unless I ask for them.'

As the teacher moved on, Rosie straightened the essay and rested her fists on it, blushing furiously.

Carrie leaned towards her. 'Never mind, Rosie. She'd have a cow if she knew what we call *her*.'

Rosie smiled briefly. Miss Blackburn's nickname was *Blackbum*. 'I know, Carrie, but these *are* Mum and Dad's names. Dad says you've got the right to be called anything you choose.'

'Ah, but your dad's not in old Blackbum's class, is he?'

'Wish he was. He'd sort *her* out, quick-sticks. Anyway, can you come to a barbecue Friday after school?'

'A barbecue? Where?'

'Our place. And will you ask Charlotte?'

'I'll have to ask my mum first. She's not keen on me going in the woods in broad daylight, never mind after school. Can Conrad come, if we get permission?'

''Course. All the Inchlake Invisibles. Tell your mum you'll be perfectly safe with my folks. I'll mention it to Peter at break.'

'Are you *chattering*, Rosemary Walk?' Miss Blackburn's voice was like a whiplash. The two girls sprang apart.

'Just borrowing Carrie's ruler, miss.'

'Hmmm.' The teacher eyeballed Rosie. 'You will be sure and give it *back*, won't you, Rosemary? Can't have things going astray in our classroom, can we?'

'No, miss.'

CHAPTER
18

'I'm really sorry, Rosie. I can't believe old Blackbum *said* that.'

'It's OK, Carrie. Not your fault. Some people are like that about travellers.' It was break-time. The two girls were in a far corner of the playing field, close to the fairy ring.

Carrie shook her head. 'Not fair though. You'd think a teacher'd know better.'

Rosie pulled a face. 'She's my gran's age, and my gran used to say this nursery rhyme to me when I was little:

> *My mother said*
> *I never should*

Play with the gipsies
In the wood.

'They used to tell kids gipsies would steal them, you see. Take them away. No wonder older people think gipsies are thieves.' She grinned. 'I bet Gran would've had a fit if she'd known her own daughter was about to become a traveller.'

'Get your ruler back, did you?' The girls turned to find Lee Kippax leering at them. He was with Carl Foxcroft and Rex Fairclough as usual.

Carrie looked at him. 'Yes I did, not that it's any of your business.'

The bully nodded. 'And is your dad going to give the pictures back too, gipsy?'

'My dad hasn't got any pictures, apple-thief.'

'Oy!' Kippax raised his fist. 'Don't call *me* a thief. Nobody calls Lee Kippax a thief.'

'Don't call me gipsy, then. The correct term is *traveller*.'

'Ho.' He put on a la-di-da voice. 'So that's the *correct* term, his hit? Haim sorry hif I caused hoffence.' His two friends guffawed.

'Go away, Kippax.' This from Carrie. 'And take your mutants with you.'

'That's not very nice, is it?' He looked at his companions. 'D'you hear what she *called* you, lads? Mutants. I'd be hurt if it was me. You know – inside. I'd want to lash out. Fancy lashing out do you, Carl? Rex?'

A slow smile warped Foxcroft's features. 'Yeah. Now you come to mention it, Kipper, I *do*. How about you, Fairy?'

Fairclough nodded. 'I like a good lash out, Foxy, you know that.'

'So what are we waiting for?' Kippax advanced on the two girls. This corner was a long way from the staffroom window. There'd be no witnesses.

'Wait.' Rosie held up a hand. 'Watch.' She stepped into the ring and shuffled backwards, arms outstretched.

The bully hesitated. 'What's your game, gipsy? How d'you mean, *wait*? Nobody tells Lee Kipp . . . huh?' He shook his head, rubbed his eyes and goggled at Rosie's empty uniform. '*Carl? Rex?* Has she just . . . am I going nuts?'

'She's vanished,' croaked Foxcroft. 'That right, Fairy?'

'Y . . . yeah.' Fairclough scowled at Carrie. 'Here – how's she *do* that, kid?'

'Never mind how I do it.' Rosie's voice came from the air above her empty clothes. 'Think about *this* – I can vanish, and I can do other things too – stuff you wouldn't believe. So if I were you I'd think twice before messing with me, or any of my friends. OK?'

'Er . . . yeah, right. Come on Kipper, let's . . .'

The trio drifted away with many backward glances. Rosie waited till they were off the field, then went visible. She grinned at Carrie.

'Useful skill, or what?'

CHAPTER 19

Halfway through Maths Miss Blackburn said, 'Are you feeling ill, Lee Kippax?'

Lee was sitting with his elbows on the table and his face in his hands. He shook his head. 'I dunno, miss.'

'You don't know whether you feel ill or not?'

'No, miss.'

'Is it the *work*? Something you don't understand, perhaps?'

'No, miss, it's not the work.'

'Well, if you're not ill and you understand the work, why aren't you getting on with it?'

'Dunno, miss.'

'No, Lee, and neither do I. If you have no

explanation for *me*, perhaps you'd care to explain yourself to Mr Beecroft. Would you?'

'If you like, miss.'

'It's not a question of what I *like*, Lee. You're here to work, and if you won't work you must expect to suffer the consequences. Go to Mr Beecroft's office at once and tell him why I sent you.'

'Come.' The Head looked up as Lee walked in. 'Now, Lee Kippax, what can I do for you?'

'Sir, Miss Blackburn sent me because I wasn't getting on with my work.'

'Really?' He gazed at the boy under beetling brows. 'And *why* weren't you working, Lee?'

'Dunno, sir.'

'Something the matter at home, perhaps? Something you'd like to talk to me about?'

'No sir. Well . . . yes, sir, but it's not about home. It's about that new girl – Rosie Walk.'

'A girl.' The brows arched. 'Not in *love* are we, Lee?'

Kippax blushed furiously. 'No, sir. She . . . can make herself disappear.'

'*Disappear?*' The Head's eyes narrowed. 'What on earth are you talking about, boy?'

'Please, sir, I *saw* her. On the field. Carl Foxcroft and Rex Fairclough saw her too.'

Mr Beecroft shook his head. 'Never mind Carl Foxcroft and Rex Fairclough. We're talking about *you*, Lee Kippax.' He clasped his hands on the desktop, sat back in his swivel chair and sighed. 'Go on.'

'Well, sir, me and . . . we were on the field, and the new girl was there with Carrie Waugh.'

'And?'

'We . . . I said something to them, sir. Sort of a joke, and then the new girl got in the fairy ring and the next thing I knew . . .'

'*Fairy ring?*'

'Yessir, there's a fairy ring. She got in it and like – vanished. There was just her clothes, sir.'

'Just her clothes? You mean, in a heap on the ground?'

'No, sir, they were standing up, but she wasn't inside them. They were like *hollow*, sir.'

'I see.' The Head leaned forward, scrutinizing Lee's features. 'Have you been *sniffing* something, laddie?'

'No, sir.'

'Have you *swallowed* something, then? A pill, perhaps? Did you take a pill from somebody?'

'No, sir, it was real, honest. We all saw it.'

'Hmmm.' Mr Beecroft sat back and folded his hands on his stomach. 'You realize that what you've told me is quite impossible, don't you?'

'I . . . *thought* so, sir, yes, but . . .'

'And yet you're convinced you saw it?'

'Yessir.'

'Well, I can't pretend I understand, Lee, so I think perhaps we'd better have your father in.'

'No, sir, don't tell my dad, please. He'll *kill* me.'

'Oh *come* now, Lee, why should your father *kill* you just because you've suffered some sort of hallucination? He might want to take you to a *doctor*, but . . .'

'I made it up, sir.'

'Ah, now that's more like it, Lee. *That* I understand perfectly.' He leaned forward. 'Feeling lazy, are we? Bit bored, so we decide we'll invent a story to liven things up a bit. Is that it?'

The boy nodded miserably. 'Yes, sir.'

'Yes, and perhaps we can get the new girl into trouble while we're about it, eh? Little bonus, so to speak?'

'Yes, sir.'

'That's what I thought.' He sat back and

regarded Lee through half-closed eyes. 'Like most bullies, Lee Kippax, you're a fool. What are you?'

'A fool, sir.'

'A fool who doesn't fool anybody, and that's a sad and sorry sight. What is it?'

'A sad and sorry sight, sir.'

'Absolutely. So you're bored, eh? Looking for a bit of a *challenge*?'

'Yes, sir.'

'All right – here's a challenge for you. Go back to your classroom, apologize to Miss Blackburn, complete the work she set and bring it to me, correct and beautifully presented at three thirty, by which time I'll have sorted out a job that'll keep you interested till, say, half past four. What do you say?'

'I don't know, sir.'

'You say, thank you sir. What do you say?'

'Thank you, sir.'

'I should think so. Now off you go. Fairy rings indeed. What *next*, I ask myself.'

CHAPTER
20

'I can't get over old Blackbum though,' growled
Carrie, 'picking on you just because you're a
traveller.' The gang was dawdling homeward.

Rosie shook her head. 'It really doesn't matter,
Carrie. Mum and Dad move on all the time so
I'm never long at one school, except in winter. I
don't care what teachers think of me.'

Peter looked at her. 'What *about* winter,
Rosie?'

The girl smiled. 'There's this showground
near Warwick, with toilets and showers and
everything. It's not used in winter so the owner
lets us stay there. Not just us, but loads of
travellers. It's no fun travelling in the middle

of winter, but it's fun at Warwick. We meet up with people we haven't seen all summer. Us kids enrol at the local school on the first of November and leave on the first of April.'

Carrie pulled a face. 'Lucky you. Must feel great, packing up and moving out as soon as the sun shines. *So long everybody – see you in November.* Wish *my* folks were travellers.'

Rosie nodded. 'It *does* feel great, but it's got a downside. No telly for instance.'

'No *telly*?' Carrie sounded horrified.

' 'Course not. We live in an old ambulance.'

'Jeez, I wouldn't be *you*.'

Rosie grinned. 'You just said you wished your folks were travellers.'

'Well yeah, but . . . no *telly*? Phew!'

'There's that,' said Rosie, 'plus sometimes it seems the world's full of people like old Blackbum.'

Peter smiled. 'And Lee Kippax.'

'Yes.' Rosie looked thoughtful. 'I've been thinking about him all day, or rather his dad.'

'His *dad*?' Peter looked baffled. 'Why have you been thinking about *him*, Rosie?

Rosie smiled. 'Remember when old

Massingberd was talking to the nurse, and she said she'd had some guy up to look at her window frames?'

'Yes, I remember.'

'She said his name was Kipper or Kepler, right?'

'Something like that, yes.' Peter looked at her. 'You mean it was . . . ?'

'Kippax, of course. He's a joiner, isn't he?'

'Yes, he is. His workshop's near Sizzlers.'

'Right. He's a joiner, and he was up at the Manor inspecting windows. He'd have to go inside to do that, wouldn't he?'

'I guess so.'

'And if there were paintings on the wall he'd see them.'

'I suppose.' His mouth fell open. 'Are you saying . . . ?'

'I'm not saying anything, Pete, except old Kippax probably saw those paintings a short time before they were stolen.' She smiled. 'Could be a coincidence, like us arriving at Inchlake just before the burglary. On the other hand . . .'

'On the other hand,' whispered Conrad, 'it might be interesting if a certain bunch of kids went invisible and did a bit of snooping round the Kippax residence.'

Rosie nodded. 'Took the words right out of my mouth, Con. What say we start tonight?'

CHAPTER
21

Twenty past six. Lee Kippax in jeans, T-shirt and trainers stands on the concrete apron in front of his parents' double garage, lobbing shots at the basketball hoop fixed over the door. Neither Foxcroft nor Fairclough have shown up to play with him, and he's bored.

As the bully lobs his forty-eighth shot (nine baskets, thirty-nine misses) something extra-ordinary happens. The ball drops through the bottom of the net but instead of hitting the apron and bouncing, it stops in mid-air. Lee stares at it. The word *hey* falls feebly from his lips. He glances towards the house, hoping his mum's at the window. His mum has already refused to believe he saw a jumper wave at him. *Tiredness,* she says. *Too much television. What you need's a few early nights.* If she was there he'd point. *Look, Mum – is* that *tiredness? Is it television?* but she's not there. His father's not around either. *Why are grown-ups never around when you want them?*

The ball's still there though, a metre above the ground. Lee stares, hoping there's a thread or something but there isn't. The stupid thing's floating on nothing, like the moon. He tries praying for a witness, but either his prayer goes unheard or the answer's no. He's moistening his top lip with his tongue when the ball chuckles.

What? Laughing at me, is it? Nobody laughs at . . .

'MUM!' Suddenly it's too much and he runs, pelting up the side of the garage. 'MY BALL'S STUCK IN MID-AIR AND IT'S LAUGHING AT ME.'

CHAPTER

22

'*Mum – my ball's stuck in mid-air and it's laughing at me.*' The Invisibles fell about as Conrad ran round the altar stone, pretending to be Kippax. They'd pulled their clothes from the recess and made themselves visible again. It was a breezy evening and they had Inchlake Ring to themselves.

'What a spack,' choked Charlotte. 'His mum'll think he's gone completely bonkers.'

Peter wiped his eyes on a tissue. 'I *loved* the way you caught that ball, Carrie. Lee's face was amazing – like a cartoon. Mind you, we didn't do much snooping.'

Rosie looked at him. 'We probably saw more than you think, Pete.'

'How d'you mean? All we did was spook old Kipper.'

'Ah, but while you were all messing about, I was using my eyes.'

'Oh yeah? And what did you spot, Sherlock?'

Rosie shook her head. 'Never you mind, Pete. I saw what I saw, and I'll tell you all about it when the time's right.' She gazed at the darkening sky. 'I think we'd better go before our folks report us missing.'

As they trudged down the footpath a chill breeze penetrated their T-shirts.

Charlotte shivered. 'There's a touch of autumn in this wind.'

'Don't say *that*,' protested Conrad. 'I want summer to go on for ever so we can keep going invisible. Can you imagine walking about stark naked in the *snow*?'

'Oooh!' Carrie hugged herself. 'It was bad enough tonight, and it's only September. We'll just have to make the most of it while we can and stop for the winter, like we do with rollerblades and biking.'

Rosie smiled. 'You'll be fed up of it by then, anyway.'

'No chance!' Conrad shook his head. 'It's the

coolest thing that's ever happened to me. I'll *never* be fed up.'

'Me neither.' Peter looked at Rosie. '*How* old did you say we'll be when it stops working?'

'Oh – twelve or thirteen. It depends. But as I say, you'll be off it long before then.'

'Not a chance. I'm gonna do it summer *and* winter while I can. I don't want to waste a second.'

It was quite dark when they reached the village outskirts. With brief *goodnights* they separated and four of them hurried towards their homes. The odd one out was Peter. He pretended to head for home, but as soon as the others were out of sight he changed course and walked rapidly towards Inchlake School.

CHAPTER
23

'Oh *there* you are, Rosie.' Daddy Bear was sitting cross-legged by the fire, plaiting strips of leather for a belt. 'We were about to call the police, report you missing.'

Rosie grinned. 'Yeah, right.' She knew he was joking.

'Tea if you want some.' He jerked his head towards the billie in the embers. 'Is anybody coming to this barbie of ours, Friday?'

Rosie poured tea into her mug. 'Oh, yes. Everybody, I think.'

Daddy Bear smiled. 'You mean Miss *Blackburn*'s planning to be here?'

'You know what I mean. All the Invisibles.'

Mummy Bear appeared, carrying a rolled newspaper. 'We thought you'd forgotten where you live, child.' She sat down. 'Any of that tea left?'

Rosie passed the billie. One of the things she liked about her parents was that they hardly ever quizzed her. Most parents would have insisted on knowing where she'd been. She nodded at the newspaper. 'Anything thrilling in there?'

Mummy Bear chuckled. 'Not really, sweetheart. I got it for the burglary, but it doesn't say much.'

'Does it say *gipsies* did it?'

'No, but it says the police are stepping up their inquiries, which probably means we can expect another visit. Tells you what they're looking for, too.'

'Paintings. We knew that already.'

'Yes, but we didn't know *what* paintings. Two Turner seascapes, worth millions.' She smiled. 'You've seen Turners haven't you, Rosie? Fantastic skies, sunlight like some great explosion, gilding everything.' Mummy Bear smiled. 'His dying words were, *The sun is God.*'

Rosie nearly said the Inchlake Invisibles were stepping up their own inquiries. Nearly, but not quite.

CHAPTER 24

Mr Rabbit was irritated. He was supposed to be meeting two guys from work at half past eight, but he didn't dare leave while his wife was in a flap. Mrs Rabbit's flap was due to the fact that Peter wasn't home yet.

'He'll be all right,' soothed Mr Rabbit. 'You know how kids are: they get playing and forget the time.'

'It's easy for you,' snapped his wife. 'All you're bothered about is your silly appointment. He could be floating face-down in the canal or lying somewhere with a broken leg for all you care.'

Peter *wasn't* floating face-down in the canal *or*

lying with a broken leg. He was sitting invisible on the settee, listening to his parents argue. They usually argued when he was in bed, so it was interesting for once to be able to hear what they were saying. Of course he knew it was wrong to eavesdrop, but so what? They'd never know.

'That's not fair, Sue,' protested Mr Rabbit. 'I care about the boy just as much as you do. *More* perhaps, since you'd have preferred a girl.'

Mrs Rabbit glared at her husband. 'Oh that's right – throw *that* in my face again. You're never going to let me forget that, are you?'

Mr Rabbit shrugged. '*You* brought up the subject of caring, Sue, not me. All I'm saying . . .'

The row grew more heated but Peter wasn't following it now. He was staring horrified at his mother while a stricken voice inside his head whimpered, *You didn't want me, you wanted a girl. You're my mum, but I could walk out of here right now and never come back and you wouldn't even care.*

His father was pacing the room, looking at his watch. His mother, her face like thunder, lifted a corner of the curtain and tutted, letting it fall. They were waiting for him, but not because they cared. He was spoiling their evening, that's all.

They hated him. He could see it in their faces. He got up and crept from the room, fighting the aching lump in his throat.

If someone's invisible, can you see their tears?

CHAPTER
25

'Lee?'

The boy was hanging about near the teachers' car park, looking miserable. He turned as Rosie spoke his name. 'What do *you* want, gipsy?'

'Just to talk.'

'What about?'

'About what you saw yesterday, on the field.'

'Oh yeah? What about it?'

'I want you to know you're not going crazy, that's all.'

'Crazy? *I* know I'm not going crazy. What makes you think I think I'm going crazy?'

Rosie gazed at him. 'You weren't looking too happy just now, Lee, and it *can* be a bit of a shock, seeing somebody vanish. And you *did* see it, that's what I wanted to say. It's a sort of trick I do, so like, you don't need a doctor or anything.'

He scowled at her. 'How about telling The Bee all this. And my dad.'

'No way. This is strictly a kid thing. No adults. If you tell anyone I'll just deny it.'

'Uh . . . I don't suppose . . . you weren't around *my* place last night, by any chance?'

Rosie grinned. 'Funny you should say that, Lee.'

'Why – *were* you?'

'Of course. Balls don't *really* hang in mid-air, do they? And they certainly don't laugh.'

The boy goggled. 'That was *you*? *Really?*' Hope in his voice, and the very beginning of joy.

'Sure it was.' She chuckled. 'I thought you said you weren't worried.'

'Yeah, well . . .' He looked uncomfortable. 'It's . . . you know . . . the way nobody believes you. You *know* you saw what you saw, but everybody's giving you funny looks and after a bit you start thinking, *Did I see it, or am I going round the twist?* It's scary.'

'Well you can quit worrying, and you can tell

Lee and Carl to chill out too, only don't try telling any grown-ups because they won't believe a word.' She winked. 'See you, apple-thief.'

'Hang on.' He looked at her. 'This trick of yours. You wouldn't ... I mean ... how about teaching me, huh? There's a million ways I could use a trick like that.'

She nodded. 'I just bet there are, and I can imagine what some of them would be, too.' She shook her head. 'Sorry, Lee. You're just not ready for that sort of responsibility. See you later.'

CHAPTER 26

'Good day, sweetheart?'

Rosie stowed her bag in the miniature cupboard under her bed. When your home's that small you've got to be tidy. She smiled up at Mummy Bear. 'Not bad. You?'

'Terrific. Sold a dozen belts and took orders for another dozen, didn't we, Daddy?'

'Sure did.' Daddy Bear grinned. 'Inchlake's crazy for hand-crafted leather.'

'Does this mean we can afford some Chinese takeaway for supper, Dad?'

'Oh, I think we might stretch to it . . . but only if you talked to Lee Kippax.'

Rosie nodded. 'I did. Told him to stop worrying.'

'And what did he say?'

'Oh, he tried to pretend he wasn't bothered but he was *really* relieved. You could tell.'

'I'm not surprised, sweetheart. It can't be much fun, wondering if you're losing your marbles. So you're friends now, are you?'

'I wouldn't say that, no.' She grinned. 'He wanted me to teach him the trick. Said there were a million ways he could use it.'

'And what did you say?'

'I told him he wasn't ready for the responsibility.'

Daddy Bear gazed at his daughter. 'And what about yourself, Rosie? Will *you* be a little more responsible from now on? No more driving bullies bonkers as a way of getting even?'

The girl blushed. 'I won't do that again, Daddy Bear. Promise.'

'Even when they call you thief or gipsy?'

'Even when they call me thief or gipsy.'

He nodded. 'Good. So, who fancies what from the Chinese chippy?'

CHAPTER

27

They'd polished off their chicken fried rice and were munching prawn crackers when they heard a car.

'Hey up.' Daddy Bear got to his feet, looking towards the sound. 'Police I expect, stepping up their inquiries.'

It wasn't the police. It was a man in a suit, looking pretty upset. Daddy Bear gazed at him. He'd never seen him before.

'Can I help you?'

The man was glancing this way and that, as though looking for somebody. He saw Rosie by the fire. 'Are you at the local school – Miss Blackburn's class?'

Rosie swallowed a cheekful of cracker and nodded. 'Yes I am.'

'So you'll know Peter – Peter Rabbit?'

She nodded again. 'He's my friend.'

Mummy Bear stood up. 'What's this about, Mr . . .?'

'Rabbit. I'm Peter's father. He didn't come home after school today. His mother's frantic. We wondered if he was here.'

'Well no, Mr Rabbit, I'm afraid we've not seen him. Have you told the police?'

'It was the first thing we did, but you know what they're like. *Shouldn't worry, sir, he'll show up at bedtime. They usually do.* It's all right for them. They don't have Mrs Rabbit to cope with.'

'No.' Mummy Bear looked at Rosie. 'Did you talk to Peter at school today, sweetheart?'

'Yes, of course.'

'And did he seem OK? I mean, not worried or anything?'

'He was a bit quieter than usual, I suppose.'

'But he didn't mention going anywhere after school?'

'No.'

Daddy Bear looked at Mr Rabbit. 'Why don't you sit down a minute, have a cup of tea? You look just about jiggered. We'll clear away, then take the van out and help you search. How's that sound?'

The man nodded. 'I could murder a cuppa now you come to mention it, and I don't suppose a few minutes'll make much difference. Thanks.' He sat down on the grass. Daddy Bear poured tea from the billie into a mug and handed it to him. Mr Rabbit sipped gratefully as the three travellers cleared up the remains of their supper and damped down the fire. It was seven o'clock and quite dark when the two vehicles swung out onto the road and growled off in opposite directions, going slowly.

Rosie pressed her face to the glass, peering out, thinking, *I hope the daft beggar's not gone invisible or there's no chance.* She turned to Mummy Bear. 'Go towards Inchlake Ring, Mum. I want to check something out.'

CHAPTER
28

Peter wasn't invisible, but tramping a country lane between high hedges at two in the morning he was pretty hard to see. Not that there was anyone to see him. The road from Inchlake to Sowerby isn't used much at night, and if he heard a vehicle he'd duck down in the ditch till it passed.

Sowerby was where Peter's grandma lived. Grandma Fox, not Grandma Rabbit. There was this family joke about Mum and Dad. Something about a rabbit catching a fox. The grown-ups laughed about it at parties but Peter thought it was daft, and he certainly wasn't in the mood for it tonight. *Shame the rabbit didn't* miss *the flipping fox,* he thought savagely, *then I'd never have been born and everybody'd be better off.* He was feeling really really sorry for himself.

It'll be OK at Grandma's. She likes me if nobody else does. She'll do me hot milk and biscuits and I'll tell her what they said. I'll ask her to let me sleep over, and not to phone Mum and Dad till tomorrow. That'll teach 'em. They'll be worried sick, even though they don't care about me really. They've always been funny about me being out after dark. He smiled to himself. *Two o'clock and they won't even be in bed. They'll stay up all night and be shattered tomorrow and it'll serve 'em right.*

He was so wrapped up in his thoughts that when a van came nosing out of a gateway he was crossing, he had to fling himself backwards to keep from being hit. He hadn't noticed the gateway or heard the van, which was travelling without lights. His violent evasive action dumped him on the seat of his pants and he sat dazed as the vehicle swung left and roared away, still without lights. *Didn't even see me,* he thought, picking himself up. *Good mind to report him, except I'd need his number and I didn't get it.* He'd noticed *something* though. Something familiar. As he knocked dirt off the seat of his jeans with both hands he realized he'd seen the van before, loads of times, but what the heck was it doing coming out of someone's driveway without lights at two o'clock in the morning? He shook his head, too tired to think about it now. Sowerby seemed pretty close when you went by car, but it was turning out to be quite a hike. He yawned and plodded on.

CHAPTER
29

'Peter Rabbit.' Miss Blackburn glanced up from her register. 'Anybody know where Peter is?'

'Miss.' Rosie held up her hand. 'He went missing, miss. Last night. His dad came to where we're parked and we went looking, but we didn't find him. I think Mr Beecroft knows about it, miss.'

A buzz went round the classroom. Lee Kippax scribbled something on a bit of paper and slipped it to Carl Foxcroft. The note passed from hand to hand till it reached Rosie. She smoothed it out and read: *What happened, gipsy? Trick go wrong, did it? What if I grass you up?* She turned the paper over and wrote, *One word from you, and stuff will happen that'll make the laughing ball seem normal. Keep it zipped, apple-thief.* She watched the boy's face turn pale as he read. He wasn't going to say a single word.

The twins found her at break-time.

'When did he *go*, Rosie? He was with us, walking home.'

'I know, but he never arrived. Must've gone off after we split up.'

'D'you think it's got something to do with . . . you know?'

Rosie shrugged. 'Maybe. His stuff wasn't up the Ring though – I checked.'

'What about *there*?' Carrie nodded towards the far corner of the field.

'No. I looked before school.'

'That leaves the ice house.'

Rosie shook her head. 'I don't think he's gone invisible. He's run off, that's all.'

Conrad pulled a face. 'Or someone's taken him. It happens.'

'Yes well . . . we've just got to hope it didn't happen this time.'

Halfway through lunch, Peter walked into the yard. Rosie and the twins ran to him. 'What *happened*, Pete? Where've you *been*?' He looked pale, but otherwise fine.

'I . . . I've been at my gran's. Bit of hassle at home. Ran off.'

'What sort of hassle?'

'I don't feel like talking about it, OK?'

'Sure. Sorted now, though?'

Peter shrugged. 'I guess. Listen.' He looked at Rosie. 'I saw something funny last night.'

'What?'

'Lee's dad's van, coming out of a driveway on the Sowerby road.'

'What's funny about *that*, Pete?'

'Two in the morning, no lights. Practically ran me over.'

'Hmm.' Rosie grinned. 'Maybe old Kippax has a girlfriend out that way.'

'Maybe. I thought I'd mention it, that's all.'

She nodded. 'Glad you did. Good to have you back, too. We thought you'd been murdered.'

Peter smiled wanly. 'I nearly was, by my gran. Half two, I got to her place. She goes, *Do your parents know where you are?* I say, *No, I want them to worry*, and she goes mental. Yells at me, phones them. I get to sleep over, but Mum comes for me at half eight. Nice as pie in front of

Gran but goes ape-shape in the car. Can't say I feel like school.'

Rosie shook her head. 'Don't blame you. Take it easy, that's all. Don't do too much, and it'll be half three before you know it.'

'Oh goody, then I can go home and have Dad yell at me. Can't wait.'

'Could be worse though, Pete. Could be floating face-down in the canal or lying somewhere with a broken leg.'

Peter stared at her. 'That's exactly what . . . you weren't at *my* place last night, were you? Invisible, I mean. Around eight?'

'What are you, *crazy*? Why would I . . . ?'

'I dunno.' He shook his head. 'Maybe I *am* crazy. I *feel* it. Everything seems . . .' His face crumpled. He bowed his head into cupped hands and cried so hard his body shook.

CHAPTER
30

Three forty-five. Rosie arrived home to find a police car parked behind the old ambulance. It was drizzling so there was no fire and nobody outside. The rear doors stood open. She mounted the step and looked in. Her parents and the two officers, sitting on chairs and bunks, practically filled the place.

Mummy Bear smiled. 'Come on in, sweetheart. Room for a little one.' She budged up and Rosie sat beside her on the bunk, hugging her bag.

One of the officers was talking to Daddy Bear. 'Before, you said you were here last night. Now you say you were out searching for some kid. Which is true?'

Daddy Bear sighed. 'I thought you meant like, late. We *were* out earlier, looking for Peter Rabbit.'

The officer gazed at the big traveller through narrowed eyes. 'I hope you're not pulling my leg, sir, because this is no joking matter.'

'I'm not pulling your leg. What makes you think I am?'

'Oh come *on*, sir. Daddy Bear, Mummy Bear, and now Peter Rabbit. Where'd you find the kid – on Mr McGregor's carrot patch?'

'We didn't find him at all. You should be out looking for him now, instead of harrassing innocent citizens.'

'He's turned up,' interrupted Rosie. 'He was at his gran's.'

The officer nodded. 'They usually are, love.' He turned back to Daddy Bear. 'So that's why you were seen driving along the Sowerby Road at eight-fifteen last night – you were looking for Peter Rabbit?'

'Not me, Sergeant. That'd be my wife and young Rosie. I was with the kid's dad in his car.'

'I see. And the only thing you were interested in last night was finding Peter Rabbit?'

'That's correct.'

'So the name Sowerby Old Hall means nothing to you?'

'Sowerby Old Hall? Not a thing, Sergeant. Should it?'

'That rather depends, sir.'

'On what?'

'On whether you're fond of ancient Greek sculpture. Fond enough to nick a three thousand-year-old life-size bronze statue of Poseidon from the middle of an ornamental pond.'

Daddy Bear pulled a face. 'Ancient Greek sculpture? I can take it or leave it, Sergeant. Mostly I leave it, because as you see . . .' He indicated the snug compartment with a sweep of his brawny arm. 'We don't have a lot of room here for life-size statues, of Poseidon or anybody else.' He grinned. 'Of course you're welcome to search the place if you suspect the thing's cunningly concealed behind a false wall or something. Far be it from me to obstruct a police officer in the execution of his duty.'

'Very droll, sir, I'm sure.' The sergeant stood up. 'We'll be on our way.' He smiled tightly. 'Wouldn't want to keep you because you never know – you might have to go out looking for Noddy or somebody. G'night, sir.'

113

CHAPTER
31

Rosie got up and followed the officers out.

'Excuse me?'

'What is it, miss?'

'Sowerby Old Hall. Has it got like a gateway in a high hedge so if you were walking you wouldn't see a car coming out till it was practically on top of you?'

'It might have. Why? Been there, have you?'

'N-no. We might have passed it last night though, me and Mum.'

'Very likely, if you were on the Sowerby road. See anything suspicious, did you? Loiterers, parked motor?'

'No. We were looking for . . .'

'I know. Peter Rabbit. Listen. If you do see or hear anything, you'll be sure and let us know, won't you?'

''Course I will. G'night.'

'OK if I go out after tea, Mum?'

Mummy Bear was mashing potatoes while her husband set the table. She nodded. 'I suppose so, sweetheart, but it's not a very nice evening. Something important to do, have you?'

'I think so, yes. I'll try not to be late.'

By six o'clock it was windy as well as wet. She didn't fancy the climb to Inchlake Ring so she used the fairy ring on the school field, packing her clothes in a plastic carrier bag which she hid in the long grass, weighted down with a stone. It would be dark soon, and it was unlikely that anyone would visit the field tonight.

The wind drove a cold drizzle that plastered her hair to her scalp and made her shiver as she hurried towards the Kippax home. This was why she'd decided not to involve the others – they'd have been half-frozen and ready to give up before the job was done.

The place was in darkness. No car stood on

the drive. When the security floodlight snapped on in response to Rosie's movements, the ring of raindrops round the basketball hoop became a circlet of diamonds. The light didn't worry her. In fact it made her task much easier, and if some busybody neighbour wondered what had triggered it and came to take a peek, he'd see nothing. *If old Kippax had a guard dog instead of a floodlight*, she thought, *it would be a different story.*

She circled the house, triggering another light round the back. There was a garden shed with a window in the side. She wiped off rainbeads and peered in. The light helped, but the shed held only a clothes-spinner, some tools and a motor mower. No life-size statue of Poseidon. *Who the heck's Poseidon anyway?*

She tried to see into the house, but all the curtains were drawn. That left the garage. The double garage. *Plenty of space in there, but no window. Drat!*

She was standing, shivering a bit and wondering what to do, when she heard a car approaching. Powerful headlights slashed across the driveway as a BMW turned in. Rosie sidestepped as the car came growling up the drive, and seized the opportunity to peer inside the garage when its doors swung up automatically and the headlights illuminated the interior. She glimpsed a tall, angular object draped in a shroud of shiny black plastic like a giant bin-bag. *That could be a statue,* she told herself. *A life-size statue. It's Daddy Bear's height. A peek under that plastic's what I need. Just a peek.*

She wasn't going to get it though. As she stared, the car rolled into the garage and the door began to swing down behind it. If there'd been time to think, she wouldn't have done the crazy thing she now did, but there wasn't. The door was half down when she dashed forward, ducked, scuttled under the descending rim and jumped clear. As the garage door clicked shut, the car doors opened and three people got out. She was trapped with the family Kippax.

CHAPTER
32

'Are we watching *The Simpsons*, Mum?' Lee hovered by the door which led from the garage to the house as his parents unloaded the car.

'You can watch in your room. Your dad's got somebody coming in a few minutes.'

'Who?'

'Never you mind. Here – take these through.'

Lee took two bulging carriers from his mother. 'Who's coming? Why can't I see 'em?'

'Lee.' Mr Kippax frowned at his son. 'Don't argue with your mother, OK? Put that stuff in the kitchen and go upstairs.'

'Yes, Dad.'

Lee went through the door. Rosie, motionless

against a breeze-block wall, watched as Mr and Mrs Kippax picked up their stuff and followed him. Should she go too, or stay here? Would they lock the door and if they did, was there a way she could escape once she'd seen what was under that plastic?

I've got *to stay, haven't I? Take a peek in the bin-bag,* then *worry about getting out.* Laden with carriers, Mr Kippax followed his wife through the door and pushed it closed with his bottom. Rosie heard a latch click home, and at the same instant the garage was plunged into total darkness.

Drat! Never thought of that. No window. Can't see a hand in front of my face. Don't know where the switches are. Why didn't I bring a torch, *for Pete's sake? (Because it'd look a bit funny, that's why – a torch floating along the street all by itself.) Still, I should've been prepared in some way.*

Gotta do *something. Can't just stand here freezing. Move.* Where, *though?* She frowned in the blackness, trying to remember the layout of the place. There was a board. Pegboard painted white with tools racked up on it, somewhere to her right. Under the board was a bench with a vice and a power-drill. Shelves below, full of stuff. A lamp, perhaps. A torch. Matches would do. *Have to search by feel but that's OK – I've probably got all night.*

She crabbed right, keeping the breeze-blocks at her back. *Go slow. Don't trip. Don't knock anything over.* When she thought she'd travelled far enough she raised her right arm and felt for the board. It wasn't there. *On a bit, then. Slowly, slowly. Now, try again. Nothing. It's here somewhere though, unless I imagined it. Wish Daddy Bear was here. Shut up. There – I've found it. Smooth and cool, just like me. Now for the bench . . . there. And underneath, down here somewhere . . . all sorts of rubbish. Careful then. Lift things one by one, feel 'em, put them on the floor. That way you won't be looking at the same stuff twice. Looking at! If only.*

Time passed. She couldn't identify most of the items her groping hands found, but none of them was a torch or lamp. She'd cleared the top shelf and made a start on the lower one when she heard a click. The lights came on. Mr Kippax, in the doorway, growled an oath as he spotted the stuff on the floor. Rosie shrank away as he strode towards her, murder in his eyes.

CHAPTER 33

Lee laughed out loud and slapped his knees as Bart Simpson pulled down his jeans and mooned the Prime Minister of Australia while a band somewhere struck up *The Star-Spangled Banner. Mega! Way to go, Bart. Best episode ever, this.*

'Lee!'

Oh-oh. 'Yes, Dad?'

'I'll give you "yes dad". Get down here *now.*'

Oh heck – now what have I done? 'Coming, Dad.'

'What you been playing at, eh?'

Lee gaped at the stuff all over the garage floor. 'Wasn't *me*, Dad. Never left my room.'

'Don't lie to me, boy.'

'I'm not. I haven't been in here, Dad. Honest.'

'So who *did* this? Your *mother*? The Invisible *Man*?'

'I dunno, Dad, but it wasn't me.'

'Oh, wasn't it? Well I'll tell you one thing – it's *you*'s going to put it all back, and you'd better be quick about it. I've somebody coming any minute and he'll not see *my* place looking like a tip. Go on – get it sorted before I kick your backside.'

Not fair. On his knees on the concrete floor, stacking stuff under the bench while *The Simpsons* performed to his empty room. *Why do I always get the blame?* He wished he had Bart's guts. He'd run through to the kitchen where Dad was putting the kettle on for his visitor, drop his jeans and moon the miserable so-and-so. Better, he'd wait till the mysterious visitor was actually *here*, drinking tea in the front room, and do it to the pair of them. Yeah, *that*'s what old Bart'd do. *Who did this, though? Somebody must have. It wasn't like this when we got back from Safeways. What if somebody broke in? Is still here?* He glanced around, moistening his lips with his tongue, but the garage was brilliantly lit. No murky corners, except . . .

122

He gazed towards the angular object under its black shroud. *Could be hiding under there with whatever it is.* Trouble was, he didn't dare go look. Not because he was scared of what he might find, but because he was scared of his father. *What's under that sheeting's none of your business, boy. Understand?* He'd said that months ago, when the first mysterious shape had appeared, and Lee knew he meant it. It wasn't the actual words so much as the dangerous light in the man's eyes as he spoke them. Lee knew that light. The black sheeting had covered many an intriguing item since then and Lee had stayed well clear. You didn't mess with Bob Kippax when he got that light in his eye.

The Invisible Man. Lee drew in a sharp breath, peering about him. *What if...?* He moistened his lips again and croaked, 'Rosie? Rosie Walk, are you here? Did *you* do this? Say something, for Pete's sake.'

No, don't.

CHAPTER
34

Rosie stood beside the statue of Poseidon, holding her breath till Lee decided she wasn't there and went back to stacking away the stuff she'd got out. Now the lights were on she could see she'd groped in vain. There was no flashlight. No matches.

It *was* a statue. She'd lifted a corner of the giant bin-bag while Lee was busy and seen a greenish foot and the shaft of what might be a spear. She didn't know for sure it was Poseidon, but it'd be a strange coincidence if it was some other statue after Peter's midnight encounter with Kippax's van in the gateway of Sowerby Old Hall.

So I was right. Kippax senior's our thief. I bet he lifted those two Turners from Inchlake Manor too. So. All I have to do is get out of here, go visible and tell the police. That'll teach 'em – case solved by prime suspect. Prime suspect's kid anyway.

Her train of thought was derailed by the sound of a motor. Lee shot a glance towards the garage door and began to work faster, but the door to the house opened and his father strode through.

'Leave that now. Go to your room and stay there till I say you can come out. Move.'

Lee straightened up, scuttled past his father and vanished into the house. *Maybe I should follow,* thought Rosie, but old Kippax moved to a box on the wall and thumbed a green button. The garage door swung up. Rosie grinned. *Panic over. I can leave now whenever I want to.*

Under the floodlight stood a van. It had reversed up the driveway. Now it came scrunching into the garage. It wasn't the blue Kippax van which had nearly squashed Pete. This one was red, and pretty ancient. Rosie tiptoed over to the house door so she could watch and not be in the way.

Two men got out.

'Bit late,' growled Kippax. 'Thought you'd blobbed.'

The driver shrugged. 'Traffic, squire. God!' He'd spotted the bin-bag. 'I'd have hired a ruddy elephant if I'd known it was this size. Solid bronze and all.'

Kippax shook his head. 'Hollow. Just over a tonne. Piece of cake, *and* you get a cuppa when it's loaded. Not many people'd look after you like I do.' He went across and started ripping away the polythene. The driver and his mate joined in. In seconds the statue stood revealed – six feet of gleaming muscle wearing a crown of seaweed and brandishing a trident, his feet buried in a drift of torn plastic. Rosie nodded to herself. *Of course. Poseidon's another name for Father Neptune and here he is, folks. Why doesn't somebody pass by right now and spot him?* She slitted her eyes, peering down the floodlit drive-way. *Oh, right. Hidden by the van. Crafty swines. I wonder . . . can I get to school, go visible, run to the police station and get back here in a patrol car before they load up, drink their tea and drive away?*

I can give it a flipping good try.

CHAPTER
35

'Now then, miss, what can we do for you?'

'I need to speak to Detective Sergeant Springer. It's urgent.'

'Oh, aye?' The constable scrutinized Rosie from rat-tail hair to sodden trainers. 'You look half-frozen. Are you all right?'

'I'm fine. Look – I know where that statue is but they're shifting it. It'll be gone in a few minutes.'

'Statue?'

'Yes, you know. The Greek one. Poseidon, from Sowerby Old Hall. Sergeant Springer questioned my dad about it, said I was to let him know if I saw anything.'

The constable pulled a fat ledger towards him and picked up a pen. 'Can I have your name, miss? Name and address.'

'Rosie. Rosie Walk. We're travellers, parked on that bit of the old Cleeston road by Inchlake Woods.'

'Aah, right.' The officer nodded. 'You're one of the Three Bears, aren't you?' He smiled. 'Baby Bear, I suppose. Well, Baby Bear, I'm afraid Sergeant Springer's not on duty tonight. Comes on at eight tomorrow morning. You could try then.'

'Tomorrow *morning*?' Rosie was outraged. 'That statue's being loaded on a van *now*. It could be in Timbuctoo by morning. Let me talk to whoever's on duty.'

'*I'm* on duty, miss. Constable Stables. Talk to me.'

'I *have*, but you don't seem to believe me.'

'That's because you haven't given me much to go on, miss. Where exactly *is* this statue, and how come *you* know about it?'

'It's in Mr Kippax's garage, and I know because I was there. I saw it.'

'Mr Kippax's garage?' The constable gazed at her. 'D'you mean *Bob* Kippax, the joiner?'

'Yes. His son's in the same class as me.'

'Is he now? And what were you doing up there, miss? It's a long way from the woods.'

'I was . . . investigating.'

'Investigating? Playing at private detectives, you mean?'

'No, I wasn't *playing*. Mr Kippax was up Inchlake Manor just before those paintings were taken, *and* his van was seen near Sowerby Old Hall last night.'

'Seen?' The constable stared at her. 'By *who*, may I ask?'

'It's *whom*.'

'What?'

'You say *whom*, not *who*. And it was Peter Rabbit.'

'Peter Rabbit.' He sighed. 'You're sure it was Peter Rabbit *whom* saw this van, and not Squirrel Nutkin or Bart Simpson or Alice in Wonderland?'

'Peter Rabbit's *real*. He's in . . .'

'Don't tell me. The same class as you, right?'

'Yes.'

The officer sighed again. 'Listen, miss. I don't know if you've heard, but there's a crime wave all over the country. The police are pretty

stretched trying to cope with the genuine stuff.
What we *don't* need is a lot of hassle from kids
called things like Baby Bear and Peter Rabbit,
with overdeveloped imaginations and too little
to do. And now I'll have to ask you to run along,
because I'm very busy. G'night, miss.'

CHAPTER
36

'Hi, Pete. All right?' Thursday morning, just before the buzzer.

Peter nodded. 'Not bad, thanks.'

Rosie smiled. 'For someone who nearly got run over by thieves, eh?'

'How d'you mean, thieves?'

'The place you were passing when the van nearly got you was Sowerby Old Hall, right?'

'I haven't a clue.'

'Well it was. And that same night, by a strange coincidence, a statue was pinched from the grounds of Sowerby Old Hall. And by an even stranger coincidence, that statue later showed up in old Kippax's garage.'

The boy goggled. 'How the heck do you *know* all this, Rosie?'

She told him about Sergeant Springer's visit to her home, and her own to the Kippax residence. She was explaining how she'd got herself locked in the garage when Carrie and Conrad joined them and she had to start all over again.

When she'd finished, Carrie said, 'Why didn't you *tell* us you were investigating? We could have come with you. We're supposed to be a gang, you know.'

'I know and I meant to, but it was so *cold*. You'd have hated it.'

'*You* managed.'

'I'm used to it. Thing is what do we *do*, now the police don't believe us?'

Conrad looked at her. 'They didn't believe *you*, Rosie, 'cause you're a stranger and a traveller. If one of *us* had been there . . .'

'It'd have made no difference,' interrupted his twin. 'It's not because Rosie's a stranger *or* a traveller, it's because she's a kid. Haven't you noticed grown-ups *never* believe kids?'

Conrad pulled a face. ''Course I have, turkey.

So what do we do?'

'Get evidence. Hey Rosie – I've got a camera. Why don't we go up the Kippax place tonight and take a picture of the statue? *That*'d prove you weren't lying, wouldn't it?'

Rosie sighed and shook her head. 'It's *gone*, Carrie. I told you, a van came for it.'

'Oh, yeah. Well – couldn't we grab Lee? Force him to confess?'

'Sure, if you fancy a rumble with Rex Fairclough and Carl Foxcroft. *I* don't.'

'Hey, have you noticed,' said Conrad, 'they've all got the letter X in their names? Kippax, Rex, Foxcroft? D'you think that's why they're a gang?'

His sister snorted. 'What the X has *that* got to do with anything, you dummy?'

'I just noticed, that's all.'

'We've got a choice,' murmured Rosie. 'Either we find a way of making someone believe us, or we say it's none of our business and stop being invisible detectives.'

Carrie shook her head. 'We can't do *that*, Rosie. It's against the law to know about a crime and not tell the police, and we know about a crime *and* who did it. We've *got* to do something. Question is, what?'

The buzzer sounded as she spoke, and Rosie pulled a face. 'We'll talk about it tomorrow,' she said, 'at the barbie.'

CHAPTER
37

Three thirty-five. The twins, walking home.

'Hey, Con?'

'What?'

'Old Kippax. He's got that yard near Sizzlers, right?'

''Course. What about it?'

'Well, we've investigated his house but not the yard. It's piled up with all sorts of junk, and then there's the buildings. He could hide a flipping *elephant* there and nobody'd know.'

'There's no elephants missing.'

'You know what I mean, dummy. Those paintings might be there. I reckon we ought to take a peek.'

'You could be right. Mention it to Rosie tomorrow night.'

Carrie shook her head. 'I'm not talking about Rosie, Con. I'm talking about you and me. What's wrong with the two of us taking a look by ourselves?'

Conrad looked at her. 'You mean like, go invisible without Rosie? Or would we do it visible?'

'Invisible, you donkey. We'll use Inchlake Ring. It'll work just the same without Rosie.'

'Yeah I know, but like . . . I prefer to have her around in case something goes wrong.'

'Like *what*, for Pete's sake?'

'Well, like if we went invisible and couldn't get back. You know – walked round the ring and just stayed invisible?'

'It won't happen, and if it did I don't suppose there's anything Rosie could do about it. I say we do it today, straight after tea.'

'I'd want to think about it first.'

'Chicken.'

'It's not that. I just don't like rushing into stuff.'

'Chicken.'

'Shut your face.'

'Chicken. I'll go by myself.'

'You can't.'

'What'll you do, chicken-licken – tell Mummy?'

'No.'

'Keep me in an armlock all night?'

'Don't be daft.'

'Come with me then.'

'I . . . oh, what the heck. All *right*, but don't blame me if we both end up invisible for ever.'

Carrie grinned. 'You're a hero, Con. I always said so.'

CHAPTER

38

It was dry, but a spiteful wind whipped the bleached grass round the feet of the ancient stones and drove flocks of ragged clouds across the sky. Conrad shivered.

'Flipping freezing.'

His twin nodded. 'Wait till you've no clothes on.'

'Oooh, don't. Think I'll go invisible first, *then* strip off.'

'Good idea.' There was nobody about. The pair positioned themselves and began walking backwards. '*Does* feel strange without Rosie. You were right about that.'

'Want to change your mind?'

'You wish!'

They completed the circle. Conrad looked down at himself. 'Think it's worked?'

''Course it has, you turkey. Let's get our stuff off. It'll be dark in an hour.'

'You start. I'm just going to take my clothes for a walk.'

'What's the point? There's nobody to see.'

'I don't care. I'll *pretend* there's someone. The Bee.'

'You're a nut.'

Carrie crossed to the stone with the recess, unzipping her top. She was shrugging it off when she heard a cry. Turning, she saw her brother topple backwards, arms flailing. She was about to laugh, but then the back of his head struck the altar stone with a sound like an apple splitting. He slumped sideways and lay like a rag doll, one arm cocked against the sky.

'Con? Conrad?' She ran towards him, her top flapping. He didn't move. She knelt, feeling his brow. 'Con? Are you OK? *Say* something.' *Daft stuff you come out with when you're scared.* 'Con?' *Shake him. No, don't. Not supposed to move someone who's had an accident, right?* She wished she knew first aid, not just fragments picked up from the telty. *He's knocked out. Dead, maybe. What the heck do I do?*

Fetch someone. Go visible first, of course, then find an adult. Or a house with a phone. Yeah, that's it. A house with a phone. Ambulance. We were playing. Just playing, and my brother overbalanced. I'll say that to Josh, like on Casualty. *He'll know exactly what to do. Clear the airway. Immobilize the head. All that. Yeah, but . . .*

Invisible. *She* could go visible in a minute, but what about him? *She* could see him, but to anybody else there'd just be a set of clothes. What would she tell Josh about that? *Oh yes, he's invisible at the moment. We go invisible sometimes. There is a head though, somewhere, and it's bleeding . . .*

Impossible. Can't fetch help and don't have a clue what to do myself. One thing. One possibility. If I carry him round the ring he'll go visible, won't he? Or have you got to be awake? Can but try. Then if it works I can get somebody. I know they say don't move the patient, but . . .

'Come on, Con love. Up we go.'

CHAPTER
39

It was unbelievably difficult. Flopping and lolling, the helpless Conrad felt like a tonne of mutton. It took Carrie more than a minute to drag him backwards, heels trailing, to the edge of the ring. She kept expecting somebody to show up and see her apparently struggling with a very heavy set of clothes. *What the heck am I gonna say? Oh, I just thought I'd take this stuff to the Oxfam shop but I seem to have come the wrong way.* Yeah, sure.

It was when she started trying to move the unconscious boy *forward* that it got really hard. She couldn't hook her hands under his armpits and drag him like before, because they'd both be going backwards. She had to sit him facing forward, then haul him to his feet and sort of *push* him in front of her. His head rolled to and fro on his chest, his arms waved about and his feet kept getting tangled up with hers. She couldn't do it in one go, it was far too tiring. Every few metres she'd stop, let him slide down till he was sitting, and squat behind him panting for a few seconds, her head on his shoulder. *What if it doesn't work – if you've got to do it non-stop?* It was no use thinking about that, or about the harm she might be doing by lugging him about. Somebody could turn up at any minute.

She'd forgotten where she'd started, so it was only the appearance of their faint shadows on the ground which told her she'd succeeded. She'd carried him right round, and it had worked. They were visible. She glanced at her watch. Five past seven. It had taken her nearly twenty minutes. Her twin was still unconscious but she could feel him breathing, which was a relief. Now she must leave him and seek help, though she was exhausted enough to fall down on the grass and sleep. She cradled his head and gazed into the pale, still face. 'Con, I've got to

CHAPTER
40

As the twins were being rushed to hospital, a really terrific idea popped into Charlotte's head. She hadn't seen the others for a few days and was sitting on her bed, wondering whether they were having invisible adventures without her. She could hear a siren somewhere in the distance. *Some poor soul off to hospital, God love 'em. I could go to school invisible.*

Just like that. What an ambulance siren had to do with going to school invisible she'd never know but that's how it happened, and the more she thought about it the more fun it promised to be. In fact she hardly slept that night, she was so excited. Friday morning she left home half an hour early and went the long way round so she'd pass Inchlake School. The yard was still deserted so she ran onto the field. The ring of little toadstools was exactly where Rosie had told her it was. She stepped in, walked carefully backwards and went invisible. Undressing quickly, she checked to see she was casting no shadow. Then she stuffed her clothes in her sports bag and hurried to the hawthorn hedge which bordered part of the field. Kids were drifting into the yard. She put the bag down, kicked it right under and piled dead leaves and rubbish in front of it. When she was satisfied it wouldn't be seen she straightened up and strolled back, wondering what the kids would think if they knew there was a girl with nothing on in their midst.

She arrived at Holy Family with ten minutes to spare. It was great, loitering by groups of her classmates, earwigging. Just before nine Teresa Walsh said, 'Hey – anyone seen Spider?' Spider was Charlotte's nickname. Then the bell rang.

'Charlotte Webb?' Ms Weekes was doing the register. She looked up. 'Anybody seen Charlotte this morning?'

'No, miss.'

'No, miss.'

Charlotte, perched on a corner of the teacher's desk, smiled. Ms Weeks was looking right through her.

Marked absent, she didn't go into assembly. Instead she reclined on two giant beanbags and had a snooze. When the class returned, she sat in her usual place and trod on Toby Coughlin's foot under the table.

Toby winced and glared at Teresa Walsh. 'Give up, you spasmo!'

'What?' Teresa was indignant. 'I didn't *do* anything, you leper. *Ouch!* Miss, *tell* him, miss, he stamped on my foot for nothing. Oh, miss, it kills.'

'Toby Coughlin . . .?'

'I *didn't*, miss, it was her who stamped on *mine*. Oh, oh, I'm *crippled* miss, honest.'

'All right, that'll do,' rapped the teacher, 'from *both* of you.'

When everybody was busy Charlotte got up, crept to the board and scrawled a rude word in large letters. She returned to the beanbags and waited. After a minute Cecilia White noticed. Her gasp made everybody look up.

'Oh, miss, look on the board. It says . . .'

'I *know* what it says, Cecilia White, thank you very much.' Blushing furiously, the teacher strode to the board and rubbed out the word. 'Who wrote that? Was it *you*, Kevin Regan?'

'No way, miss.' The boy grinned. 'I didn't know you spelled it like that, miss.'

Charlotte chuckled, the sound masked by general laughter. Who said school was a drag? It was going to be a wonderful day.

CHAPTER
41

It all started to go wrong at half past eleven. By then Charlotte had done a few things, like giving Kylie Reid's hair a sharp tug during Silent Reading, tripping Esau Enright in P.E. so that instead of sailing over the vaulting horse he performed a spectacular sliding dive *under* it, and transferring the terrapin from its tank into Ms Weekes' coffee cup. The kids were enjoying an unusual morning and the teacher was starting to look a bit wild-eyed when there was a shy knock on the classroom door and Split le Beau walked in.

Charlotte couldn't believe it at first. She goggled. *Split le Beau, lead singer with Dead*

Ringer? It certainly *looked* like him, but why the heck would . . .? *Ah!* She recalled a rumour she'd heard, that Split's real name was Douglas Murgatroyd and that he'd once been a pupil at Holy Family.

'Douglas!' Ms Weekes stood up, smiling, as the world-famous superstar approached her desk. 'To what do we owe *this* honour?' A buzz of excitement rippled through the class, especially among the girls, most of whom had Dead Ringer posters on their bedroom walls.

The lad grinned. 'I was in the area, miss, so I thought I'd drop in. Hope I'm not wrecking your lesson?'

'No, no.' Her old pupil was making her blush harder than Charlotte's rude word had. 'It's lovely to see you, Douglas. Or should I be calling you Split?'

The lad shook his blond head. 'Oh no, miss – that's just for the fans.'

'I suspect you've got a few fans among these children, Douglas. Just look at their faces.'

Split grinned at the gobsmacked class. 'How you doing?' Sighs and moans rose from the young people. His grin broadened. 'How about

I sign some jotters or something?' He glanced at the teacher. 'That all right, miss?'

'Of course.' She smiled. 'I fancy I'd have a riot on my hands if I said no.'

In a flash, everybody had their jotters out and were scraping back their chairs.

Ms Weekes held up a hand. 'Just a minute!' Reluctantly they subsided. 'We'll do this properly, a table at a time.' She looked at the superstar. 'Why don't you sit at my desk, and we'll form a queue?' She stared at the class. 'An *orderly* queue.'

And so it was that over the next twenty minutes, every kid in the class got to chat briefly with the scrummy Split le Beau and collect a personalized autograph. Every kid in the class *except* Charlotte Webb, who had to hover at the back of the room, drooling.

He departed at five to twelve with a grin and a wave, having turned down the teacher's invitation to stay for a school dinner. The class, twitchy with residual adrenalin, tidied up under Ms Weekes' eagle eye and filed out to lunch. The teacher remained for a moment, gazing at the signature on her own jotter, then swept off towards the staffroom, leaving Charlotte cold, distraught and alone.

She crept unseen out of school and down the road. *Oh, Split – why today, of all days?* There was a spiteful wind, and it would be at least four hours before she could retrieve her clothes. She pulled a face. *Invisibility? You can keep it.*

CHAPTER
42

It stayed dry, so the barbie went ahead as scheduled. While Rosie was at school the two Bears built the oven out of stones borrowed from a nearby crumbling wall, then combed the woods for kindling and sawed up a fallen tree, stacking the logs beside the oven. In the afternoon they drove into Inchlake and loaded up the ambulance with sausages, steaks, fish, rolls and fizzy drinks. They bought firelighters too, just in case. When Rosie got home everything was ready.

'Looks great, Dad, Mum. The kids're going to love it.'

Mummy Bear smiled. 'What time did you tell them, sweetheart?'

'I said around seven. That OK?'

'Sure. Change into jeans and jumper, then help me carry chairs out. There'll be seven of us, is that right?'

'There's supposed to be, but I'm not sure about Conrad. He fell last night and knocked himself unconscious. They kept him in hospital overnight so he wasn't at school today.

'Oh, dear. What was he doing to fall, Rosie?'

'Messing about up Inchlake Ring with Carrie. She thinks he'll come if his mum and dad'll let him.'

'I don't think *I*'d let him come, sweetheart. Concussion's a funny thing.'

'I bet *he*'s not laughing.'

'You know what I mean.'

At five to seven the Waugh family Volvo appeared. Carrie got out, then to Rosie's delight Con emerged with a bandage round his head.

Daddy Bear bent by the driver's window. 'We'll keep an eye on the lad, Mr Waugh.' He smiled. 'Unless you want to stay, of course. You'd be very welcome.'

The twins' father shook his head. 'Thanks, but

my wife's got a job for me. I'll collect them around ten if that's all right.'

'Certainly is. See you then.' He gazed after the car as it crunched away down the bit of broken road.

It was five past seven and the kindling was ablaze when Peter arrived on foot. 'Hey, you'll never guess who *I* just saw.'

Rosie looked at him. 'Who?'

'Split le Beau.'

'Did you heck.'

'I *did*. He drove right past me in this fantastic Merc.'

Conrad shook his bandaged head. 'What would Split le Beau be doing in a dead hole like Inchlake, you moron? It was someone who *looked* like him, that's all.'

'No it was *him*, as close to me as you are now. He looked just like his poster.'

Carrie pulled a face. 'It's dark, Pete. You could've been mistaken.'

'He's not,' said Charlotte flatly. She'd arrived unnoticed by her friends, though Daddy Bear had seen her.

'How do *you* know?' asked Carrie. 'Did he

pass *you* in this fantastic Merc as well?'

'No, he came to school.'

'Yeah, right.'

'No, he *did*. He used to go there, that's why. Miss Weekes was his teacher.' She could see they didn't believe her. 'He signed everyone's jotter, so there.'

Conrad looked at her. 'Show us, then.'

'He didn't do mine.'

'Aaah, *see*.' He looked at the others. 'She's giving us a load of old cobblers.'

'No I'm *not*. I couldn't get mine done because nobody knew I was there. I was flipping *invisible*, see?'

'You went to school invisible?' Carrie chuckled. 'Wish *I'd* thought of that.'

'Well *I* wish I hadn't.'

Conrad nodded, fingering his bandage. 'Know what you mean, Spider. Not always fun, eh?'

'Hey, you kids!' Daddy Bear called from beyond the flames. 'Anyone ready for a sausage?'

Everybody was.

CHAPTER
43

'They were clever, those neolithic people,' said Daddy Bear. 'They knew hundreds of things we don't – things that are lost now. Forgotten. But they couldn't understand why invisibility didn't work any more once they reached the age of twelve or thirteen. It could have been useful to them in all sorts of ways. Hunting. Avoiding enemies. They kept walking widdershins round fairy rings but it never worked. They thought maybe they needed a *bigger* circle 'cause they were bigger, so they built stone circles like Inchlake Ring but that didn't work. They tried other shapes, such as spirals and swastikas and mazes. They carved 'em on rocks, cut 'em into the turf and built 'em out of stones but it was all no use. They never cracked it because it can't be done, but they left all these elaborate experiments behind and that's where some of our most famous patterns were copied from. It's why we have mazes. You know, those puzzles in comics where there's a tangle of lines and you've got to find your way to the centre without crossing one?'

'Wow!' Conrad swigged Coke from the bottle. 'I never knew *they* had anything to do with the Stone Age.'

Daddy Bear chuckled. 'Oh, you'd be amazed how much we owe to those guys, Con. Their forest clearance and farming formed a lot of our landscape. The countryside wouldn't look the way it does if they'd never lived.' He smiled round the circle of tired faces. 'They were here and then they were gone, and we must go too.'

There were mumbled protests as the big traveller clambered to his feet. 'Aw – can't we just have five more minutes, Daddy Bear? Three then? One? Fifteen seconds?'

He shook his head. 'Everything comes to an end, kids. Even the good stuff. Mr Waugh will be along any minute, and then Mummy Bear'll drive Charlotte and Peter home while Rosie and I clear up here.' He grinned. 'Hands up if you've had a rotten time.'

There were no hands.

CHAPTER
44

Nothing much happened for a few days after the barbie. Saturday they all slept late. Sunday they discussed what they should do about Kippax and decided gloomily that there wasn't much they *could* do without proof. Conrad's bandage came off on Tuesday. Thursday night Charlotte brought Teresa Walsh's jotter to prove Split le Beau *had* visited his old school, and then it was Friday. Friday's always the best day at school, but this one was going to be really special.

While the children were at lunch a blue van came nosing into the yard. On its side in white letters were the words ROBERT KIPPAX – JOINERY &

GENERAL PROPERTY REPAIRS. Kippax senior was an old pupil of Inchlake School, and the van called about once a month to drop off a sack or two of nogs and offcuts the children could use in Design and Technology. When he saw the vehicle arrive, Mr Beecroft strode into the dining area and chose four volunteers to carry the wood into the DT store. One of these volunteers was Rosie.

The driver was sliding sacks out of the back of the van and dumping them on the tarmac. Rosie was relieved to see it wasn't Kippax himself, but one of his workers.

'Right.' The Bee organized his posse. 'Two to a sack. Four sacks. That's two journeys each. *Don't* try to carry one by yourself – there are no Arnold Schwarzeneggers at Inchlake School.' The volunteers tittered dutifully. The Bee smiled at the driver. 'Thanks. And thank Mr Kippax for me, will you?'

'I will. Tarra.' The man swung himself into the cab and drove off, anxious to be clear of the yard before the kids came swarming out.

Rosie's partner was Carl Foxcroft. She'd tried to team up with the other girl, but The Bee had suggested girl-boy pairs and he was the boss.

Carl smiled nastily as they lugged their burden through a side door. 'You wanna take this lot home, gipsy. Make a lot of clothes-pegs, this would.'

'We don't do pegs, you moron, and we're not gipsies.' She eyeballed him. '*You* could use it though – fill that empty space between your ears.'

As they dumped the heavy sack on the floor it collapsed sideways, spilling a few nogs. Rosie squatted and scooped them up. As she went to tip them back in the bag, she saw a strip of gold-painted wood sticking out. It was pretty, with a pattern of curly leaves glistening along its length. She pulled it out. It was about a metre long. At either end was a short, ungilded section cut at an angle. It reminded her of . . .

'What is it?' Carl Foxcroft peered at the strip.

Rosie shrugged, though her heart was racing. 'Dunno. Nice though, isn't it? Think I'll have it.' She straightened up.

The boy leered. 'I'll get you done.'

Rosie stared at him. 'You've got a short memory, Foxy. Remember that day on the field?'

'What day? What you on about, gipsy?'

'Oh come *on* – you remember. Clothes, *walking by themselves*?'

'Oh . . . yeah.' He looked uncomfortable, as though he'd been reminded of something he'd rather forget. 'What about it?'

'*This* about it, moron.' She thrust her face into his. 'That stuff's nothing – absolutely *nothing*, compared to what'll happen if you grass me up to The Bee. You got that?'

'Uh . . . yeah. Yeah, OK.'

'It *better* be OK.' She hid the gilded strip in a corner, right at the back of the store where it was dark. She leaned it against the wall behind a stack of cardboard boxes. The place wasn't kept locked. She could slip back later and get it.

She smiled to herself, going back for the second load. *I could be wrong I suppose, but I think that strip's what we've been waiting for. I think we've got our proof.*

CHAPTER
45

Bob Kippax was agitated. He kept coming outside, glancing around and going back in the
Portakabin which served as his office. After a bit
he called across the yard to a young man in
overalls who was stacking new timber. 'Where's
Leonard gone with the van, Malcolm?'

The young man slid a board onto the stack
and turned. 'It's the first of the month, Mr
Kippax. He's down the school with the offcuts.'

'Ah, right. Where did he take 'em from, d'you
know?'

'Well – all over, I suppose, same as usual. I
mean, this delivery had just come in so I wasn't
taking much notice. Why?'

Kippax ignored the question, gesturing towards a dilapidated shed. 'Did he take anything out of there?'

'He might have. Like I say, I wasn't watching him. I was busy.'

'OK.'

He was halfway up the office steps when he heard a motor. The van swung into the yard. He waited while the driver parked and got out. 'Leonard?'

'Yes, boss?'

'The stuff for the school. Did you get any of it from the shed?'

'A few bits, yeah.'

'Any *old* stuff?'

'Don't remember, could've been. Why – is something up?'

'The frames from those flipping pictures're in the shed, only there's a piece missing. You've not taken *that* to the school, have you?'

Leonard shook his head. 'Don't think so, boss, but I couldn't swear to it.'

'You couldn't *swear* to it?' Kippax glared at the hapless driver. 'You know what'll happen if you have and somebody spots it, don't you?'

'Sure, boss, big trouble. Want me to go back there and check?'

'Oh yeah. What you gonna say? *Excuse me Mr Beecroft, d'you think I could take a look at those off-cuts I brought just now – I might have put stolen property in by mistake?* No.' He continued up the steps. 'You've screwed up enough for one day, Leonard. Get back to your work. I'll sort it.' He went in the office and picked up the phone.

CHAPTER 46

First period after lunch one of the little kids knocked on the classroom door and came in. 'Please, miss, can Lee Kippax go to the office? He's wanted on the phone.'

Miss Blackburn sighed. 'Yes, all right. Off you go, Lee, but don't be all afternoon.'

'Hello?' The school secretary had left the office to give him privacy.

'That you, Lee?'

'Dad. What's up?'

'Listen. Do you know where they keep the wood?'

'What wood?'

'The wood I send round for CDT or whatever they call it nowadays.'

'Oh, yeah. The DT store. It's sort of round the side of the . . .'

'I don't want to know how to *find* it, you dummy. Can you get in there?'

'Well yeah, but . . .'

'It's not locked?'

'No.'

'Right. Get yourself round there, *now*. Leonard's just dropped a load off. Four bags. I want you to search 'em. You're looking for a piece of picture frame, gilded, about a metre long. You got that?'

'Yes, Dad, but I can't go now. We're in the middle of Geography.'

'I don't care if you're in the middle of the Pacific Ocean, you cretin. Get round there and find that wood, unless you want to be visiting me in jail.'

The prospect of seeing his father locked up for a year or two appealed to the boy, but he was a dutiful son. 'I . . . I'll do my best, Dad. Tarra.' He hung up.

I can't go now. Old Blackbum'd come looking for me. She'd think I was either dodging her lesson or nicking from the store. Both, probably. I'll go at half three.

'Finished?' asked the secretary as Lee emerged.

'Oh – yes, miss. Thanks.'

'Not trouble at home, I hope?'

'No, miss.' He returned to the classroom. *Dad's trouble is, he panics. Never get anywhere if you panic.* He picked up his pencil, made a dot in the middle of the Pacific Ocean and smiled.

Me.

CHAPTER
47

Half past three. The moment Miss Blackburn dismissed the class, Rosie headed for the DT store. She'd just slipped inside and pulled the door to behind her when it opened again to admit Lee Kippax. He scowled at her.

'What's your game, gipsy?'

Rosie looked at him. 'What's yours?'

'The Bee sent me to tidy up in here.'

'Oh. Well, I was just looking for something.'

'What?'

'Doesn't matter, it's not here. See you.' She slipped past him.

Blast! Now what do I do? She went out into the yard. *The Bee never sent him, he's after that bit of wood. That's why he was wanted on the phone. Our bit of proof's about to disappear.*

She glanced around, hoping to spot Peter or the twins among the departing pupils but it seemed they'd already gone. All she could think to do was hide behind the bike shed and watch the door till Lee came out. Maybe he wouldn't find what he was looking for.

He didn't. At a quarter to four he emerged empty handed, looking glum. Rosie's heart soared. *You can't hide a metre of wood in your pocket, but I can't* believe *he missed it.* She watched as the boy trailed disconsolately out of the yard, then slipped back inside.

It was there, in the corner where she'd propped it. She grabbed it, peeked round the door to make sure no cleaner was about and left the building, intent on catching up with Peter and the twins. She was in such a hurry that she jogged right past the phone box without noticing that Lee was inside, and that he'd clocked her.

CHAPTER
48

As Rosie approached the phone box, Kippax senior was blasting his son's eardrum. 'OF *COURSE* SHE WAS LOOKING FOR THE SAME THING AS YOU, YOU DAFT LITTLE GROMMIT. SHE'S PROBABLY IN THERE RIGHT NOW SHOVING IT IN HER . . .'

'Dad!' The boy goggled through the glass. 'You're *right,* she's just gone past with it in her hand.'

'WELL WHAT YOU *WAITING* FOR, YOU PILLOCK? GET *AFTER* HER – GET IT OFF HER. GO *ON!*'

'OK, Dad. I'm off.' Lee slammed down the handset and burst from the kiosk. Rosie was disappearing round a curve, pumping the bit of frame up and down like a relay runner with the baton. He raced after her.

At first he did well because the girl didn't know she was being chased. She jogged up the road, swerving through kids dawdling home-ward, expecting any minute to see Peter and the twins in front of her. Lee, going full pelt, was closing the gap. Then, when he was no more than twenty metres behind, some daft kid swerved into his path and they collided. 'Hey!' cried the startled child. 'Why the *heck* can't you watch where you're going?' Normally Lee would have taken time out to flatten him, but Rosie had heard the kid's cry and glanced back. As soon as she saw Lee she knew what he was after and put on a spurt. Raised in the country, she could run like a hare. In seconds the gap had widened to thirty metres, then forty, then fifty. The thought of what his dad would do to him if he let the gipsy get away acted as an accelerator to Lee, who pounded after her.

Rosie was lean and fit but Lee was desperate and she couldn't shake him off. She was blow-ing hard and getting a stitch in her side when she saw Peter and the twins ahead.

'Hey, wait!' They recognized her voice and turned. Rosie lolloped up to them, gasping. 'This.' She held out the gilded wood. 'Proof, I think. Off up the Manor . . . make sure. Grab *him.*' She jerked her head towards Lee, who had spotted her in company and slowed. 'Give me a start, OK?' She staggered on.

Lee swerved into the middle of the road to avoid them. They spread out to block him and he ran roaring at Carrie, thinking she'd chicken out. She didn't. As he charged her she lowered her head and rammed him in the pit of his stomach. He collapsed onto his knees, hugging his middle while his face turned purple. As he toppled sideways the two boys threw themselves on him, pinning him to the ground. Carrie glanced up the road. Rosie was well clear but limping. They'd need to hold Lee for a minute or two but it wasn't a problem. Badly winded, the bully lay spread-eagled like a dead starfish under Con and Pete. She'd just permitted herself a faint smile when she heard the sound of a motor moving at speed. A blue van came zooming up the road and screeched to a halt. The driver's door was flung open. Bob Kippax emerged looking murderous. He strode towards them.

CHAPTER 49

'GERROFFIM! LERRIMUP!' The two startled boys rolled off their victim as his father stormed towards them. Lee sat up, wrapped his arms round his stomach and rocked. Kippax glared down at him without sympathy. 'Where's that bit of wood, you useless lump – don't tell me you didn't *get* it?'

'I . . . she ran off, Dad.'

'She's a GIRL, you plonker. Girls don't *run*, they flap about. Which way's she gone – where does she *live*, for Pete's sake?'

'She's not gone home,' blurted Peter. 'She's . . .'

'SHUT IT, PETE!' This from Carrie.

Peter clapped a hand to his mouth. 'S . . . sorry.'

Kippax eyeballed him. 'Where *has* she gone, boy? Spit it out or I'll shove two fingers up your nose and pull an eyeball down.'

'I . . . I dunno, Mr Kippax.'

'Yes you do. I bet it's the *police station*, isn't it?'

'No.'

'Good.' The man smiled tightly. 'So what does *that* leave?' He frowned, thinking.

Peter and the twins started backing away, ready to run. Lee had risen to his knees and was knocking dust off his uniform. He gave his father a sulky look. 'Bet *I* know where she's off to.'

Kippax senior glanced at his son. 'Come on then, Einstein – enlighten us.'

'What – in front of *them*?' Lee nodded towards the three children.

Kippax glared at them. 'Make yourselves scarce NOW, or I'll report you for assault. GO ON!' He watched as they pelted up the road, then turned to his son. 'OK – where? And *do* get up out of the dirt, you boneless twit.'

Lee clambered to his feet. 'That bit of frame – it's off a painting, isn't it? One of those nicked from the manor.'

''*Course* it is. Why else would I care if someone got hold of it? Where's she *gone* with it?'

'Up the Manor.'

'The *Manor*? What the heck *for*?'

'To make sure.'

'Make sure of *what*, you prawn?'

'To make sure it *is* off one of the Turners. She'll show old Miss whatsername – Massingberd – then take it to the police.'

The man's eyes narrowed. 'D'you think so? D'you think she's that smart – a ruddy *gipsy*?'

'She's not a gipsy, and she *is* pretty smart. I'd bet a year's pocket money that's where she's gone.'

Kippax chuckled unpleasantly. 'You just *did*, sunshine. Come on.' He strode towards the van.

CHAPTER
50

They ran till Lee, his father and the van were way behind. When they stopped, panting and swiping sweat from their foreheads, Conrad gasped, 'D'you reckon Lee *does* know where Rosie's gone?'

Peter shrugged. 'Dunno. His dad called him Einstein, but Frankenstein's more like it. *I* don't see how he could know.'

Carrie pulled a face. 'He might *guess* though, and I wouldn't want to be Rosie if he does. I think we'd better get up there in case she needs help.'

Peter looked at her. 'How could *we* help, Carrie? You saw what old Kippax is like when he's mad. We need the police.'

Carrie sighed. 'Yes, Pete, I *know* we need the police, but the police need evidence and *we* haven't got it – *Rosie* has. We're *kids* – they wouldn't believe a word we said.'

'So *you* suggest something.'

'OK.' She gazed at the two boys. 'I know we can't stand up to Kippax as we are *now*, but it'd be different if we were invisible, right?'

'Ugh!' Conrad shivered. 'No more invisible for *me*, Sis. Not after what happened to me last time.'

'You were being a div last time, Con. Messing about. There'd be none of that this time.' She turned to Peter. 'Tell him, Pete.'

Peter pouted. 'Actually I'm not keen myself, Carrie. Stuff can happen when you're invisible. Bad stuff. I vote we tell a grown-up – our parents or The Bee or somebody.'

Carrie snorted. 'Waste of time, Pete. Nobody'd *believe* us. Listen – we're supposed to be a gang, aren't we? Well – *aren't* we?'

'Yeah.'

'I suppose.'

'And the point about gangs is that members stick together, right? Help one another.'

'Uh . . . yeah.'

'Hmmm . . .'

'Well then – *Rosie*'s a member, she could be in trouble – in *danger* – so it's up to us to help her. Am I right?'

'Haaar.'

'Umph.'

'Is that a *yes*, or what?'

'Ah . . . yeah.'

'Uh . . . mmm.'

'Well come *on* then – let's go.'

'Where?'

'The *ice house*, of course. How *else* do we go invisible? Move.'

'Just when I'm *dying* for my flipping tea,' groaned Conrad.

CHAPTER
51

Charlotte dawdled along the road feeling glum. *OK, so it's Friday. No school tomorrow, but it's also the first weekiversary of not getting Split le Beau's autograph, so it's a bummer. Everything's a bummer, and invisibility's the biggest bummer of them all.* She aimed a kick at a drift of fallen leaves, turned the corner and stopped dead. Right in front of her, not twenty metres away, stood a long silver Mercedes. Beside it, leaning on its gleaming roof, smoking a cigarette, was Split le Beau.

She couldn't believe it at first, but stood gaping as her jaw dropped and her knees turned to jelly. *It isn't him. It can't be. He's a superstar. He wouldn't hang around this dead hole for a week.* She was gathering her courage to go up to him and say, *Excuse me, but has anybody ever told you you look just like Split le Beau?* when he noticed her and smiled across the polished roof.

'Hello.'

'Huuu . . . uuu . . . hello. Is it *you*, really?'

'It's me, really.' The cigarette wagged as he spoke. 'What's *your* name?'

'Charlotte. Charlotte Webb. I . . .' She'd been about to say *I saw you at school*, but changed it to 'I missed you at school. Last week. I was away.'

He grinned round the cigarette. 'Shame. Still you've caught me now, haven't you?'

'Uh . . . yes.' She giggled, feeling her cheeks flame. 'Can I . . . would you mind . . . ?' Fumbling with her bag.

'An autograph?' He smiled. 'Don't worry about paper, I've got some snapshots some-where.' He opened the driver's door and stooped to the map pocket. Here y'are.' He rested the photo on the roof and spoke the words he was inscribing as Charlotte moved closer. 'To Charlotte – sincerely – Split.' He looked up. 'What's today's date?' She told him in a hoarse whisper and he added it with a flourish. 'There. That all right for you,

Charlotte?' He handed her the glossy photo.

She glanced at it, nodding. 'It's . . . fabulous, Split. Fabulous.'

The superstar chuckled. 'Good. Well – better get on. Got an appointment at four. 'Bye, Charlotte.'

'Oh, yes. Bye, Spl . . .'

He was swinging himself into the driver's seat when there was a sound of running footsteps and Rosie came tearing round the corner. She saw the car, then Charlotte, and as he leaned across to get the door, she saw Split le Beau. 'Wha . . .?' The shock broke her rhythm. She came to a panting halt, looking from Charlotte to Split and back to Charlotte. 'Charlotte, how the . . . what're *you* doing with . . . oh, heck!' She glanced behind, held up the bit of frame. 'Gotta go. The Manor. Kippax behind. I'll phone later. See you.' With a last yearning glance in Split's direction she ran on, sweat glistening on her forehead.

His chuckle diverted Charlotte's attention from her friend's flight. 'What was all *that* about?'

'Oh . . .' She shook her head. 'It's nothing. That's Rosie. We're just . . .' She broke off as a blue van came screeching round the corner. Split had to slam his door to keep it from being torn off its hinges as the vehicle swerved by. He shook his head. 'Crazy folk you got around here, Charlotte. You better . . .'

'*Please*, Split . . .?'

He looked up at her. 'What *is* it kid? What's going on?'

'I'm not sure, but I think that van's after Rosie. D'you think you could . . .?' *Never get in some-one's car*, hissed her mind, but surely . . . Split le Beau . . .

'Sure, hop in.' He leaned across, opened the passenger door. 'Did I hear your friend mention the Manor?'

'Yeah, that's where she's gone I think.'

'Weird.' He put the car in gear and it shot forward, slamming Charlotte back in her seat.

She looked across at him. 'What?'

'The Manor. It's where my four o'clock appointment is. Hold on.' They screamed round a bend and sped on.

Charlotte felt unreal.

CHAPTER
52

Made it, and still no sign of Kippax. Rosie hurried up the driveway and mounted the mossy steps. The yellow Polo was parked at the bottom, which meant the nurse was here again. Rosie hoped she wouldn't stop her seeing Miss Massingberd.

There was a bell-push screwed to the door. She thumbed it, glancing over her should. *Come on, Flo Nightingale – it's urgent.* She knew it would be the nurse and not Miss Massingberd who came to the door. It felt like ages before she heard footsteps. The door opened a crack and the nurse frowned down at her.

'Yes?'

'Can I see Miss Massingberd for a minute, please? It's *really* important.'

'Oh it *is*, is it? Why?'

'It's about her pictures. The ones that were pinched. I know who did it.'

'*Do* you, now?'

'Yes, look.' Rosie held out the piece of frame. 'I think this is off one of them. If Miss Massingberd could just . . .'

'I'm sorry. Miss Massingberd is unwell, and besides she's expecting somebody at any minute. If you come back tomorrow . . .'

'It'll be too late.' She heard an engine down by the road, knew it was Kippax. 'Here.' She thrust the gilded strip at the woman. 'Take this to the old lady. She'll recognize it.'

She was halfway down the steps when the nurse called after her. 'What's your *name*, little girl?'

'Rosie.' She flung the word over her shoulder without stopping. 'Rosie Walk.' She could see the van through thin autumn foliage. Another second and the driver would see *her*. She heard the door close behind her as she raced for the shrubbery.

Too late. She was less than halfway there

when the van overtook her, slewing to a stop in
a spray of gravel. The driver's door flew open
and Kippax baled out. Before she had time to cry
out or change direction he'd grabbed her. A
brawny arm circled her neck, a rough palm
clamped her mouth.

'OK, gipsy, where is it?'

'What?' She kicked and writhed and tried to
bite his hand.

'You know what. *Come on – what you done with
it?*' The arm round her neck tightened. She
began to choke. Through her tears she could see
Lee in the passenger seat, watching. The
pressure eased a fraction and she croaked, 'I
don't know what you mean.' She prayed the
nurse was showing the strip to Miss
Massingberd right now.

'YOU KNOW ALL RIGHT.' He was shouting,
shaking her. 'SPIT IT OUT OR I'LL THROTTLE
THE LIFE OUT OF YOU!'

She was choking. Flashes in her eyes like stars
exploding and blackness round the edges, flood-
ing in. A hand gripped her flailing forearm. A
hand she couldn't see. A *third* hand, and a voice
hissed in her ear, *The ice house. Say it's in the ice
house. Carrie*'s voice.

She battered the brawny arm with both fists. The stranglehold loosened. 'Well?'

'The ice house. I hid it in the ice house.'

'That's better.' The arm was removed. Rosie sucked in air as the man grabbed a fistful of hair to steer her by. The blackness was receding. 'Come on – show me.'

She was stumbling through a tangle of neglected shrubs, her head thrust forward. Twigs scraped her face and Kippax kept treading on her heels as they waded through wet leaves. He was panting with exertion as he shoved her along, sounding like a big dog. The ice house came in sight through the trees. What would she do when they reached it? What would *Kippax* do to her when he realized she'd lied?

Hey, Rosie, stay cool. Carrie whispered to you, right? That means the Invisibles're here. Or does it? What if being strangled makes you hear things that aren't really there?

Well if that's the explanation you'll be hearing 'em again, dude. Real soon.

CHAPTER
53

The nurse punched in the number, heard the first ring and handed the receiver to the old lady. Miss Massingberd held it to her ear, gazing at the strip of gilded wood on the table. Somebody picked up.

'Hello? Is this the police? Good afternoon, Constable Stables. This is Miss Massingberd, calling from the Manor. That's right, the Manor. There's been a . . . development, I suppose you'd say, in the matter of my stolen paintings. Well, a child rang my bell a few minutes ago, claiming to know who took the paintings. A child, yes. A little girl. She handed my nurse part of a picture frame and it *is* from one of my Turners. Her name?' Miss Massingberd shot the nurse an enquiring glance and lip-read the woman's response. 'Walk, apparently. Rosie Walk. Oh, you *know* about her? *Is* she a gipsy? I really couldn't say, Constable – didn't see her myself. Oh, I don't think . . . she'd hardly come up here and ring the bell if she was the thief, would she? Her *father*? But why would a daughter . . . did you say *double bluff*? I'm afraid I'm not familiar with the term. Oh, I don't think she's here *now*, Constable. The nurse told me she ran off. Come by all means if you think that's best. You can collect the bit of frame if nothing else. Good, then I'll see you presently. Goodbye.'

The nurse put down the receiver. 'On their way, eh?'

The old lady nodded. 'Keen, our Constable Stables. Very. Doesn't like gipsies by the sound of him.' She looked at the nurse. 'Did the child look like a criminal to *you*, my dear?'

The nurse pulled a face. 'No, but then if criminals *looked* like criminals there'd be no need for detectives, would there?'

190

CHAPTER 54

Rosie knuckled her eyes and sniffled. No fun, being lowered into darkness by your hair. It hurts, plus she was dead scared. Who wouldn't be, alone in an abandoned ice house with a guy like Kippax? Even down here he didn't relax his grip. Her scalp felt tender, as though it was lifting from her skull. He squeezed and she cried out, the sound echoing eerily in the damp blackness.

'Right, gipsy . . . where is it?'

'This way.' She chose a direction at random, creeping forward. *Where are you, Carrie? Do something for goodness' sake,* quick. *Don't let me die down here.*

They must have been halfway across the floor when Kippax gasped and swiped at something in the blackness. The movement caused a tug on Rosie's hair and she yelped.

'What *is* it?'

'Dunno.' The man peered into the gloom. 'Bat, maybe. Never mind.' He shoved her forward, but they'd taken only two paces when there was a sharp scraping noise and a match flared. Kippax started violently. 'WHO'S THERE?' The flame steadied, trembling in a draught. He couldn't see the hand that held it. 'WHO IS IT?'

'Nobody, Robert Kippax. Nobody at all.' Rosie's heart soared. The voice was distorted by echo and disguised to sound like a ghost's, but she recognized it and smiled. Good old Pete.

Kippax was shaken. Rosie felt the hand that held her hair start to twitch and bit her lip to keep from giggling. The match dwindled and died. The man continued to stare at the place, seeing a greenish blob. 'I'M WARNING YOU, WHOEVER YOU ARE,' he bellowed. 'NOBODY MESSES WITH BOB KIPPAX. *NOBODY.*'

'That's *right*, Robert Kippax, and that's exactly who *I* am. Nobody. Look.' A second match, in a different spot. This one moved up and down, from side to side, back and forth, its little globe of brightness revealing no part of the speaker. The tremor in Kippax's hand grew more pronounced. *Any second now*, thought Rosie, *he's gonna forget I'm here and let go.* For the moment though he went on deploying the bully's weapon, bluster.

'YOU'LL PAY FOR THIS. YOU CAN'T STAY IN HERE FOR EVER AND WHEN YOU COME OUT I'LL BE WAITING.' He stared into the blackness, breathing heavily. Rosie stood absolutely still, saying nothing.

'You are *so* wrong, Robert Kippax. *So* wrong. We *can* stay here for ever, for this is our hoo – ooom.' Rosie nearly burst out laughing as Carrie made the word *home* sound like the hoot of an owl. Its echo had scarcely faded when the voice continued. 'You have entered our home uninvited, and for that you must be punished.' At this point somebody evidently struck the man because he swung round with an oath and threw a punch, relinquishing his hold on Rosie's hair to do so. She stepped lightly to one side and was lost to him at once.

'HEY!' The frightened bully spun round, groping for his victim. Three metres away Rosie stood holding her breath, knowing she was as safe from him now as if she were on Mars. 'DON'T THINK I CAN'T SEE YOU, GIPSY, 'CAUSE I CAN. GET HERE – *NOW!*'

'Temper, Robert Kippax.' Con's voice, hollow in the gloom.

Kippax turned slowly on the spot, unable to tell where the speaker was. 'YOU DON'T SCARE ME WITH YOUR SILLY PUT-ON VOICE, SO DON'T THINK IT.'

'You *sound* afraid, notwithstanding, and I see you've lost your prisoner. Perhaps you should leave.'

'I'M NOT LEAVING TILL I GET WHAT I CAME FOR.'

'You'll get what you came for if you *stay*, Robert Kippax – that I promise you.'

'HOWDYA MEAN?'

'Stay, and find out.'

'I'm not. I'm going, but I'll be waiting, and when you come out I'll make you wish you'd never been born.' He moved towards a faint luminescence which marked the position of the entrance. 'THAT GOES FOR YOU TOO, GIPSY.'

It was then the laughter started. Demoniacal laughter from every direction at once, echoing and re-echoing till it seemed the ice house harboured a thousand devils. He *tried* to go slowly. *Tried* to hold on to what was left of his dignity, but the laughter woke a memory from the distant past – a film he'd seen as a kid, set in a creepy Victorian asylum. He hadn't slept properly for weeks after watching that film, and he'd nursed a secret dread ever since – a dread of losing his mind and being dragged off screaming to a place like the asylum in that film. He quickened his pace, muttering to himself as the laughter ricocheted inside his skull. *I'm not mad, just because I see matches that strike themselves and hover in the air, like . . . like Lee with that ball. (Runs in families, madness.) I'm not mad. Not mad.* He stumbled sobbing towards the light and looked up and there, gazing down at him, was the most famous pop star in England.

Of course he was.

CHAPTER
55

Split's Mercedes had swung through the gateposts of Inchlake Manor seven minutes behind the blue van. It could have been two minutes and Kippax might never have got Rosie as far as the ice house, but Split missed the turn first time and had to backtrack. By the time he and Charlotte came in sight of the house there was no sign of either the joiner or the girl, but the van was there with its engine ticking over and Lee in the driver's seat. The boy's jaw dropped when Split stuck his head through the window.

'Rosie – where is she?'

'Uh – *you*. You're just like that singer – you know – Split le Beau?'

'I *am* Split, and I'll split *you* if you don't answer my question. WHERE'S ROSIE?'

'You're *him*? Wow! Uh . . . Rosie said the *ice house*, whatever that is. They went that way.' He flapped an arm towards the shrubbery.

'They?'

'Huh?'

'You said *they*.'

'Yeah – Rosie and Dad.'

The star straightened up and looked at Charlotte. 'The ice house?'

'Yes, I've been there.'

'Lead on then, *quick*.'

They heard the racket in the ice house long before they reached it. 'Oh God!' sobbed Charlotte, 'he's *murdering* her.' They pelted towards the mossy dome and round it, reaching the doorway in time to see a dishevelled Bob Kippax scrabbling to haul himself out. Peals of ghastly laughter pursued him as he heaved his top half clear and flopped gasping on the grass. Noticing a crocodile shoe three centimetres from his nose he looked up, straight into the face of Split le Beau.

'Aaaagh!' He writhed on the ground,

kneading his eyes with his fists. 'I'm *not* mad, I tell you. *Not* mad.'

As the ice house laughter dwindled, there was a crashing in the bushes and a policeman burst out yelling, 'I *know* you're in there, Miss Walk. Come out quietly and you won't get . . .' He skidded to a halt, goggling at the man on the ground. '*Bob?*'

'I'm *not* mad!' Kippax got up on his hands and knees and crawled towards the officer. 'They're *real*, those matches. I *saw* them strike themselves. Wave themselves about. And the voices, laughing at me. *They*'re real too.' He grabbed his school chum's ankles and rested his forehead on the toecaps of his boots. 'Don't let them put me away, Steve. Prison, yeah – I *deserve* that, but not the . . . not the *loony* bin.'

As Kippax blubbed on Stables' size elevens, there was movement inside the ice house and Rosie stuck her head out. 'Oh hi, Charlotte. Glad you could make it. Everyone else is here.' Three grinning faces appeared. Carrie recognized Split and squealed. '*Oooh*, look who it is. Shift yourself, Rosie – let me get *at* him.'

Split leaned towards Charlotte and whispered in her ear. 'Your friend seems to be OK so I'll slip away before I'm mobbed. Nice meeting you, Charlotte.'

As the superstar vanished into the bushes, Bob Kippax plucked at the constable's trousers.

'See – *he*'s real, isn't he, and you wouldn't expect to see . . .' He gestured to where he'd last seen Split, but he wasn't there. Stables glanced where Kippax was pointing, then down at his friend. '*Who*, Bob? Who wouldn't you expect to see?'

Kippax appealed to Charlotte. '*Tell* him, kid. Tell him Split le Beau was here.'

Charlotte frowned and shook her head. 'Split le Beau? *Here*? I'm afraid you're *seeing* things, Mr Kippax.'

CHAPTER 56

Hometime, Friday October 22nd. Three weeks had rolled by since the exciting events at Inchlake Manor. The weather had grown colder, especially first thing in the morning. Next week the clocks would go back. Winter was closing in.

'So, children.' Miss Blackburn stood up, rubbed her hands together and smiled. 'The time has come when we must all say goodbye to Rosie Walk.' She beamed at Rosie, who had become something of a heroine since her ordeal in the ice house. 'I don't suppose we'll ever see you again, Rosie, but I'm sure everybody here joins me in wishing you good luck in the future.' A murmur of assent rippled round the classroom. Every eye was on Rosie. She blushed.

'Thanks, miss. Thanks, everybody.' She smiled. 'I don't expect to miss Inchlake very much, because we travellers see so many places and after a while they all run into one. I never miss schools either, but I do miss *people*, and I know I'm going to miss all of you.'

The children, unsure what response was called for, smiled and nodded. Then somebody at the back started clapping. Everybody looked round. It was Lee Kippax, who'd become a different boy – a *happier* boy since his father went away. He looked at his classmates, growled 'Come *on* then,' and everybody began to clap, including the teacher. Rosie picked up her bag and hurried from the room with flaming cheeks.

'Good send-off or what?' grinned Peter, when they were clear of the school.

Rosie groaned. 'I nearly *died*. Trust old Lee to embarrass the heck out of me at the last minute.'

Conrad chuckled. 'He's *grateful* to you, Rosie. Life's really opened up for him since that awful dad of his went to prison.'

Rosie grinned. 'Not very nice for *him*, though.'

'Oh, I don't know,' said Carrie. 'He'll be

relieved it's prison and not the loony-bin after what he saw in that ice house.'

'*Thought* he saw,' amended Peter, straight-faced.

Carrie nodded. 'That's what I meant.'

'Boo!' They jumped and squealed as Charlotte sprang from behind the phone box.

Rosie goggled. 'How'd *you* get here so quick?'

Charlotte grinned. 'Told Miss Weekes I had a dentist appointment. Well – I couldn't let you go without saying goodbye, could I? Besides, I've got a secret to tell.'

Carrie looked at her. 'If you tell, it'll stop being a secret.'

'No it won't. It'll be a secret known only to our gang. I know you won't spread it around.'

'What is it, then?'

'It's about Miss Massingberd.'

'Miss *Massingberd*?' Conrad groaned. 'Can't be anything exciting then, can it?'

'Well – it's about Split le Beau as well.'

'Miss Massingberd and Split le Beau? Don't tell me . . . they're getting married, right?'

'No, you smeghead! Miss Massingberd's off to live with her sister in Devon, and guess who's buying the Manor?'

'Not . . .?'

'Yes – Split le Beau. Isn't that great? We'll see him all the time.'

Rosie shook her head. '*I* won't.'

'Oh no, you *won't*, will you? I never thought of that.'

'Well don't let it worry you, Charlotte. I'm used to meeting people and then not seeing them any more.' She smiled. 'It's about to happen right now, in fact.' They'd reached the old Cleeston Road. Rosie stopped. 'Listen, you guys – long goodbyes screw me up, so it'd be cool if you didn't come any further with me, OK?' There was a break in her voice, as though she was talking round an aching lump. The others looked at their feet.

Peter murmured, 'I thought I'd come and say thanks to your folks, Rosie. Y'know – for the barbie and that.'

Rosie shook her head. 'No need, Pete. They know you enjoyed yourself.'

'Yeah, but . . .'

'It's not what people *say*, Pete – it's what they *do*. They only had to look at you to know the evening was a hit.'

He nodded. 'OK.'

'You off tonight?' asked Conrad.

Rosie shook her head. 'Tomorrow, first thing. We'll be at Warwick by lunchtime.' She looked at the four of them. 'Think you'll go invisible now and then?'

'Hmm.' They shuffled, looking down.

'Winter's coming on,' mumbled Conrad. 'Too cold. Next spring, maybe.'

Peter nodded. 'Yeah, spring.'

Carrie said nothing at all.

Rosie nodded, knowing they'd never be invisible again. Some things sound fun till you try them, then you discover the downside. 'I'm off, then. Think of me sometimes if you don't forget.'

Peter blinked and swallowed. ''*Course* we won't forget, how could we?' His smile was watery. 'The Inchlake Invisibles. We'll *always* be your gang, Rosie, even if we never meet again.'

Rosie smiled. 'Great last line, Pete. Look after one another. 'Bye.'

THE END